The Games We Play...

A Novella

WRITTEN BY:

K.D. HARRIS

STREET KNOWLEDGE PUBLISHING

Published by: **Street Knowledge Publishing**
Street Knowledge Publishing
P.O. Box 345
Wilmington, DE 19899

Copyright date: 2012
ISBN: 978-1-944151-08-9

The Games We Play a novel by K. D. Harris
Edited by: Navimjan Services LLC
Cover design by: Street Knowledge Publishing Services
Formatted by: Krystol Diggs
Typed from handwriting to text by: Vanessa Cooper
Female model on cover:
Male model on cover:

All Street Knowledge Publishing titles are available at special quantity discounts for bulk purchases for sales promotion, fund-raising, educational, or institutional use and book clubs.

www.streetknowledgepublishing.com

Printed in Canada

DEDICATION

FOR MY LADIES WHO FELL VICTIM TO THE
"D"

Chapter 1

If you judged me by my upbringing, I wouldn't be pegged as a bad chick. If you really knew me I would be voted most likely to end up on America's most wanted. I was far from an angel; however, my parents would beg to differ. You see when you grow up financially stable; go to the best schools and the word *no* was never in your parents vocabulary-it's inevitable that you may turn out not so great. I guess you can say that I was one of the ones who fit in the "not so great" category. I was accustomed to getting what I want when I wanted it. As I stated before *no* did not register in my mental when it was directed towards me. I solely blame my father for that.

When I was sixteen he bought me my first car, a sleek black fully loaded Lexus. By the time I graduated from Padua Academy, I wrecked two of them and was driving around in a new Audi R8 my senior year. My best friend Lilith, who I opted to call Lil for short, has been my conscience since we were in first grade. Her attempts to steer me right while I

4

headed left failed ninety percent of the time. Lilith wasn't as fortunate as we were; at least that's what she thinks. I couldn't tell. We went to the same private school, Sanford Prep, until I was transferred to Padua Academy in my junior year. Lil was a worry-wart. She thought extremely too much about shit that's not relevant; at least not in my life. What the hell did I care about the ozone layer, or what was happening on CNN. I thought CNN was Capone and Noriega. I'm joking, I know what CNN was, but I didn't give a flip about what they were talking about.

She was raised by a single mother, Ms. Laurie who happened to be our housekeeper and our second mother since I could remember. My father didn't consider her a maid, although that was her job description. She wasn't paid like one neither. I don't know too many people who were in her profession receiving an annual salary and their child sent to private school courtesy of their employer.

Ms. Laurie was like my mom, so Lil was my sister. She was raised in the hood-Eastside to be exact. She was from 9th Street two blocks down from Brown bag convenience store. Her mother was at our home from eight in the morning until six o'clock in the evening Monday thru Friday. She prepared Sunday dinner for us every week with no complaints. She was there so much...I believe she should have moved in. My mother wasn't with that at all. She was the only Queen in her Casa.

I lived a secluded sheltered life in Middletown. That was beyond the suburbs. Anything over the St. Georges Bridge was country. Our home was lovely but we were in the middle of nowhere and needed transportation to get everywhere. My parents lived a lavish lifestyle most of their acquaintances were from the hood. Let me rephrase that; my father, Kevin, acquaintances were. He was from the Eastside as well. He was raised on 8th and Kirkwood Street right next to where Cliff's convenience store used to be. His mom was one of the original crack heads and his dad was on heroin and couldn't stay out of the Smyrna Correctional Institute. My dad and Ms. Laurie went to school together. I used to think they had a thing for each other back in the day. My dad was extremely generous to her and the four kids she had by her deceased- husband. My mother thought so too and she was jealous on the low but never showed it around my father or Ms. Laurie. Lil and I noticed it though. I would joke about it all the time. Lil worried that she would make my dad fire her mother. That was a joke. My mom couldn't make my dad do a damn thing. Truth is he saved her ass.

My father was a true dream chaser. He did everything he had to do to get out the hood and make it. He now owned his own architectural firm, in addition to owning properties all over Delaware and Pennsylvania. He was living proof that a black man can make it in a white man's world. My mother Nisa was born in Sierra Leone and moved to the United

States when she was fourteen years-old. My mother's family was dirt poor and my mother was often sent to bed hungry. She worked on some old man's farm in the chicken coup down in Georgetown, Delaware. When she turned eighteen she was turning down sheets at the Sheraton in Dover. That's where my dad found her. She already had one child by then, my brother Chance, who my dad took on as his own.

That was over thirty-five years ago and if you met my mother now you wouldn't guess that she grew up dirt poor. My mother's snooty attitude usually offended people, especially if they weren't on her level. Her outrages behavior caused friction within our family. She didn't talk to her own siblings because she felt they were beneath her, now that's some foul some shit. I thank the man -upstairs that I didn't inherit her mindset. We were nothing alike henceforth when I hit puberty we stopped getting along altogether. She couldn't understand that no matter how many private schools, etiquette classes she put me in…I was still going fuck with goons.

It's something about a nigga with gunshot wounds that made my panties moist. Niggas from the city were my weakness. Let me stand corrected, not just a basic nut ass city nigga, but one that demanded authority with cash and a strong back. I didn't do foot soldiers. If you weren't the plug you weren't getting in my socket-facts! This was the reason I found myself in the clinic so much getting treated for STD's and shit; or why my tires stayed slashed back in high school. Unfortunately, those type niggas entertained several bitches-dirty bum bitches at that. After having my heart broken twice, I gave up on men and dated women for a short while, until I realized that Snoop was right when he said bitches weren't shit. So instead of focusing on relationships I focused on money, mullah, cash, or stacks. If you can't spend - I'm not in-straight- like- that.

I was somewhat of the black sheep of the family. I didn't want to live in my father's shadow like my oldest brother Chance and I damn sure didn't want to be some house wife like my sister Amelie, so I paved my own path and started my own business. I was self- made. I owned a natural hair-care products line like the first female millionaire, Madame CJ Walker. My business blew up quickly, thanks to the almighty internet. I watched YouTube like it was regular television you wouldn't believe the money you could make from the internet. All I had to do was send my product to the chicks that had the most followers and they made the money for me. Tutorial referrals on YouTube and Instagram made me six figures in six months. Shit I wasn't dumb. I knew that I wanted to be my own boss I just didn't know which avenue I was going to take. I chose correct. I am twenty-five years old and my net worth is about a half a million dollars.

"Brynn, don't you think you need to slow down with the drinks honey?" I looked at Lilith and guzzled my drink down anyway.

I paid her comment dust. It was my birthday and I was lit!

"Lil, I've reached a new milestone in my life okay so let me enjoy myself, here I am twenty-five, single, and paid can't a bitch breathe?" my mouth was another reason why my mother and I couldn't get along. I said what I wanted; whenever I wanted; fuck the formalities and shit. This was a dog-eat-dog world where everybody cussed men, women, and children.

"Ladies don't curse..." she would say.

My mother always said that I act like my father's sister Ora. I took it as a compliment, I loved my aunt Ora. My mother and my aunt Ora never got along and it drove my father crazy. My mother thought that she was better than my aunt, and my aunt stayed putting her in her place. I used to laugh my ass off as they argued while my siblings left the room and pouted. I guess they didn't find the shit funny, but I did.

When I first started my business no one wanted to help me, not even my own father because he didn't agree with my career choice. His desire was for me to go to law school, but my thing was, why would I when I was constantly breaking the law? I had to start my business from the ground up and build my own start up capitol, believe me it wasn't easy. It took a couple of trips to a few well known cellular companies to get a line of business credit under bogus names, obtain about thirty of the hottest phones for free of course; then hit craigslist and off them to the highest bidder. Shit a girl had to make moves. How they say it…faith without works is dead?

Lilith stood by my side the entire time and guided me as I weathered the storm that's why she was the COO of my company, Fleek Hair Products. Where I got that name from? You already know! That's my song. I stayed on fleek so why not name company after my character. I am my brand period. My business has been up and running for four years strong, and I am so proud of us.

"You know something Lil, my parents have been calling me asking me when I was going to settle down and get married that shit is getting on my nerves I mean who gets married at twenty-five?" as soon as the words left my mouth I regretted them. Lilith was recently married and had a six-month old son with her man of three-years, Ravon or Hov as he was called. I couldn't stand his fake gangster ass. Looking like Ceaser, not in Julius but the gorilla.

"You know I didn't mean it like that but hell I love my single life I don't need or want a man right now."

You're drunk girl let me get you home!" was all she said as she placed my arm around her neck and stumbled out of Bahama Breeze as I stumbled along the way.

Chapter 2

"Damn you sure know how to lick the icing off a cake!" I said to Shock as he sucked my pussy dry. Even though I didn't want a man in my life fulltime, I still had needs. I had a fetish for getting my pussy sucked-hoover style. I continued to watch as he expertly ate my box and I released my oils all over his face. I saw him inching his way up to me with his hard dick in his hand.

"Uh-uh what the fuck do you think you're about to do nigga? I told you all I wanted was to get my pussy sucked get that shit away from me."

I pushed him back as I sat up in the bed.

The expression on Shock's face told me that he was pissed but I didn't give a shit. "Brynn you know you're wrong but you got it ma!" he said as he stood up to retrieve his pants. I met Shock a few years back while I was down the shore in Atlantic City. He was getting a slew of money out there. He was from Philly-North to be exact. His money was long;

however, that wasn't what attracted me to him. He was humble, sweet and a goon at the same damn time. He catered to me and I was feeling that shit. I loved to dress in fine fabrics but I wasn't about to spend *all* of my hard earned money on a bunch of ridiculously priced garments because of the name on the label. That's how the white people stayed rich. Think about it, most white kids you go to school with look basic, maybe a tad bit homely. When you pull up to their crib it's like you walked into an episodes of Orange County housewives, they were living lavish. They were smart. They knew how to bargain shop too. They stayed at Marshall's and T.J Max in West Chester. That's where all the good high price shit was. I bought a cute pair of Coach Sneakers from there last summer.

I let niggas buy labels for me. Shock wasn't stingy at all. He loved showering me with gifts. I only gave him the pussy twice since during our situation. I couldn't call it a relationship. It was more like an understanding. When I needed to release some stress he was the one I called on. His tongue was talented and kept me more than satisfied. Shock was a sexy street nigga with a wild streak out of this world but when it came to me he was a sweetheart which was part of the reason I kept him around.

We were standing inside of Chipotle when I noticed this fine, sexy ass man with luscious lips and swag for days. My cousin Pam was with me and I noticed she too was checking him out; the only difference was that she was drooling over this nigga. Plain and simple Pam was a gold-digging whore that would fuck the pastor, his deacons, and the first lady if she could. Since we were kids Pam threw her pussy around like beat up rag doll, needless to say, she was the whore of the family. It started out with her fucking around with all the young boys at the church-to fucking police officers, school teachers, judges, and district attorneys. That bitch never worked a day in her life but she drove around in a hot 745 BMW and lived in a fly ass Condo in Wilmington on the Riverfront. At least she was getting more than some change for doing something strange, either way who was I to judge when I was no saint myself?

"Brynn! My pussy is thumping girl do you see him? That nigga can fuck me every way possible, and I do mean every way possible." She stressed as she licked her lips. She did the Delaware two-step and snapped her fingers. Pam was thick in all the right places like the chicks at a down south strip club. She had a cute baby doll face and she was the color of sweet caramel. She had immaculate white teeth and chin length hair that stayed flat ironed to perfection. I looked at my cousin and laughed. That's all you could do was laugh because she was who she was and didn't care what anyone thought about her.

"I'm ready to go."

I was about tired of standing in the line. I was hungry but I was over the wait.

"Bitch, we didn't even eat yet. We only got like fifteen people ahead of us." She whined.

I rolled my eyes and leaned against the wall; truth of the matter was my panties were getting moist just by the thought of what he could do to me. I don't know what the man was doing but he looked good doing it.

"Where did he disappear to? It's a must that I get his number and fuck him sooner than later, yass! My precious feline is throbbing right now."

This hoe was in the middle of Chipotle on crackerville Main Street, gyrating and moaning like a porn star. She knew damn well these white people weren't about that ratchet shit. If she kept it up Newark Police would be up in here trying to site her ass on lewd behavior. They didn't care if it was going to get thrown out of court. The only action Newark Police got was drunken University of Delaware students and the occasional racial profile stops. By the time we walked out he was long gone, but I swear he was on my mind like past due bills.

This was strange because the only thing that stayed on my mind was money. I had to get it together and fast because Brynn Nisa Davis didn't want or need a man in my life and couldn't a soul tell me anything different.

"Honey when are you going to settle down like your father and I?"

I looked at my mother and sucked my teeth and as usual she scolded me for it. "Don't you dare suck your teeth at me Brynn unless you have something stuck between them, you know that's not lady like dear."

No matter how hard my mother tried to talk proper, her African accent was still thick and heavy. You better not call her African she would lose her mind. I tell her all the time you can't run from yourself.

My mother had strong features but she wasn't like the Africans you see on television. She was high yellow with fine wavy hair. There was some jungle fever popping off over in the motherland. She was naturally flawless but she wore heavy make-up which made her look plastic. There was no need for her face to look casket fresh every day. She was beautiful; she had pretty big brown eyes with long curly eyelashes and naturally arched eyebrows. Simply put, my mother is drop-dead gorgeous and I could see how she captured my father's heart. Now my father Kevin, on the other hand was a big black man. He wasn't all that handsome but that didn't matter. He was sharp as a tack and the females loved him, especially at the church. His tall chocolate ass would come strolling in there with a fly ass designer suit and shoes; the women, and some men would fall out - it wasn't from the Holy Ghost.

I guess I was a mixture of the two of them, but I looked more like my mother than my father. Many people say that I resembled Zoe Saldana, which was bullshit. People had to always categorize people. Oh she looks like Beyoncé; oh she's shaped like K. Michele. How about you look like your damn self? I saw that shit all too much on social media. Photoshop was a bitch. If you knew what you were doing a hoe could very well, make her ass look damn near better than Bey. I looked like myself and I embraced it. Besides I was darker and had way more body than the Avatar broad. I was milkshake from Sonics thick and no bitch could fuck with it. My hair is naturally curly, one of the reasons I started the natural hair product line.

Settle down...me? Never... why would I when there is so many fine ass niggas out there that I haven't tried yet. I'll follow my Aunt's lead. She seems to be doing great!" I teased, knowing this would piss my mother off. My aunt Ora dated plenty of men, but settled down with none. She said that eventually all men cheat and she wasn't wasting her time and energy with just one. I couldn't even fault her because she was right.

"Oh mother she'll come around one day I love my husband and family." My sister Amelie purred as she held her new born baby girl Ciara in her arms. I wanted the throw my bottle of water at her head. I turned my nose up at her. I don't even know where she came from. Her and her crew entered the room. She smiled and handed the baby to her husband Felito, who was a fine Puerto Rican. Fine in looks but there was something about him that made my ass itch.

"Hey baby girl. Did you find yourself a husband yet?" my father asked taking a seat across from me. "I mean what's the point of success if you don't have anyone to share it with?" My mother and sister agreed.

I loved my dad dearly but this shit was getting on my nerve. This was not the sixties and the *Leave It Beaver* conversation was blowing me.

"Easy, when I die I'll take it with me, he better find his own way out in the world like I did and mommy who are you to talk when daddy found you?" My mother's face turned bright pink and I couldn't hold back my laugh. "Like I told you before I don't want or need a man and as long as I got my money I'll be straight."

"You shouldn't speak that way. All women need a man that's how God intended it to be." My mother explained.

"No God intended us to virgins and he is our groom. Read the book, mom." I scoffed.

"You're sickening, Brynn, really sickening." My sister said with disgust.

"Well its best that you stay away from me. I may be contagious."

I didn't see what the issue was. I was doing me. I stood up and gathered my things.

"See this is why I don't come over here like that. Y'all be on some other shit."

"Brynn, watch your mouth." My dad said.

17

My sister rolled her eyes and added her unwanted two cents, "Your mouth is so filthy Brynn this is why you can't find a good man."

I stopped what I was doing and laughed, "Girl bye! I have a slew of great men in my pocket. If I ever wanted to be exclusive with any of them I could. Like I said I'm good. Now let me go before you make me get out of character."

I turned on my heels and headed towards the door. I left them knowing that I would most likely be the topic of discussion for the rest of the day. I had other shit to do than entertain their bullshit.

Chapter 3

I was my own boss so I would go to work basically whenever I wanted to. Lilith ran the business in my absence, and like a true partner-in-crime she did a damn good job. I was planning on going in today but Pam called me and asked if I wanted go out to get something to eat at this new restaurant in the mall. I had to eat to live so I agreed. I resided out in Bear, in a newly built Craftsmen's home off of route forty. I was minutes away from the mall. She insisted on coming to get me, and I told her to call me when she got outside. Twenty minutes later I heard her car horn blowing so I grabbed my keys and walked out of the house shaking my head because I told her ass to call me not blow the horn.

I was dressed tastefully in a pair of tight True Religion jeans, a crisp white button up shirt and a hot pair of nude pointy toe Louboutin heels. My hair was pinned back in a bun and my make-up was photo shoot fresh. I opened the door to car snickered and

19

shook my head. My cousin was dressed like a high-priced whore, yet rocking the hell out of a black dress with spiked heels. She wore her hair in big curls flowing down her back and her make-up was just right I could tell that she was looking to reel in a big fish tonight.

"You look cute bitch. What you been shopping at *Whorestroms*?" I said as we pulled off listening to Bryson Tiller crooning, "Don't…"

When we pulled up at the mall it was packed as usual. Christiana Mall had become high-end within the last two years so everybody wanted to be out there. The only thing Concord Mall had to offer was Chic-Fil-A and Hollister and Tri-state Mall should have shut down years ago. I mean who still shops at City Blue? Everybody knows the Sneaker Villa was the new City Blue. Did they *not* get the memo?

Once we were inside we walked through the food court and headed towards Nordstrom's. The restaurant was across from the water fountain near California Pizza. It was a line out the door.

I stopped in mid stride. The distorted expression on my face let her know I wasn't pleased. The line was out the door resembling the one at the Department of Labor when Obama extended the time frame for unemployment checks.

"Oh God not today Brynn just sit back and relax I told Mina we'd meet her here she says she knows the owner." Mina was Pam's close friend and cool people's so I gave her a pass.

"How does she have a restaurant in the mall? I thought you had to be a chain to get up in here." I inquired.

She shrugged her shoulders and we maneuvered through the massive line. No one said a word but the looks on their faces was priceless. I was cool as long as no one tried to get fly. We found Mina engrossed in an intimate conversation with a strikingly beautiful sister that could have easily been a fashion model. She stood five feet ten inches, with pretty long legs and a pretty smile. She was clad in black J. Mendel frock dress and a sexy pair of Marc Jacobs to match. She was rocking the hell out of an asymmetrical bob and her hazel eyes went well with her brown sugar skin. When we approached the table I saw Pam studying her profile so I was the one who broke the ice.

"Hey how are you doing? My name is Brynn and this is my cousin Pam, we're friends of Mina would you mind if we joined you two?" I said it like Mina wasn't siting right there. I mean-she didn't say anything and we were all standing around looking dumb.

The woman stared at me with open eyes and smiled.

"Of course not have a seat I'm Onnie, the owner, Mina is a very dear friend of mine please have a seat both of you." Mina gave Pam and I hugs and air kisses then turned her attention back to Onnie who was still openly staring at me.

"Onnie… girl this place is beautiful I'm so proud of you I know Emilio is too." She finally took her eyes off me and gave Mina her full attention.

"Thank you girl, you know I've wanted this for a long time now I'm just happy that I have the opportunity to finally do it, and Emilio is very supportive." The décor in the place was sick, and it had an Afro-eccentric with a splash of Latin feel to it, I knew off the bat I would like this place. The lights were dim with contemporary dining furniture. There was a double door with a platinum plate next to the doors with the word elite engraved in it. I guess that was for private parties or meeting. I didn't expect to find an upscale Soul-Caribbean restaurant in this mall. This place was fit to be on 5th Avenue or Rodeo Drive.

"So what are you ladies in the mood for?" Onnie asked playing hostess. The sexy ass man we saw at Chipotle the other day walked in the door followed by two other fine niggas with pencil thin goatees and striking features. I felt my mouth watering and before I could respond Pam's slut-ass said something.

"Sweetheart, I'm in the mood for him covered in caramel and a can of whipped cream, trust me when I say this, I will drink his fucking bathwater on a summer day."

Onnie looked in the direction of Pam and smiled, "Sorry honey he's *not* on the menu let me introduce you to my *husband* Emilio."

"I can't believe that fine nigga is her husband girl I was so ready to fuck his brains out did you see his dimples? Oh I need to call up Tory so he can be waiting on me when I get home." Pam whispered pulling out her iPhone.

Having lunch with Mina and Pam was fun, and after finding out that Mr. Sexy Face from the other day was married to Onnie, the owner of the Caribbean and Soul food restaurant, the lusting over him was a thing of the past, besides he wasn't my type anyway I didn't fuck around with married men.

I went home that night, pulled out my big black dildo with the hairy balls attached and fucked the shit out of my pussy. I haven't had sex in over a year and counting. I felt that my stuff was too good to be given away to a no-good nigga so I took care of my own needs. That night I thought of Emilio as I slid up and down on my fake dick. The dildo was saturated with my cream filling, and I was on the verge of coming for the third time. I let out a big sigh of relief and passed out. That night I dreamt of getting fucked really good by Emilio in the backseat of my Mercedes, why when I constantly told myself that I didn't want a man?

***

"Lil hey girl, where's my cute god-son at? I picked him up a few outfits from The Gap." I know that Gap was old but it will never go out of style-it's classic. I'd been at Lil's two-story family home in

North Wilmington for almost an hour and just now remembered that I had some clothes in my trunk for him.

"I've been here for a while and haven't seen him yet is he sleep or something?"

"Brynn I told you three times already that he's with his father girl. Where's your head at in the clouds somewhere?"

Lil was right, I did ask her that three times already and every time she told me the same thing but for some reason I wasn't hearing her. My mind had been on sex all day and not that fake shit I had last night with my dildo but a real hard dick attached to Emilio. I was so fucking horny that I couldn't even think straight.

"Brynn is everything alright? I'm worried about you."

I snapped out of the trance I was in so I wouldn't have Lil worried about me, the girl was a worry wart for real.

"Oh yeah I'm fine how's everything between you and Hov? Are you enjoying the married life?"

When my best friend told me she was getting married a year ago I was shocked. I mean her and Hov had been on and off for a couple years now, mainly because he couldn't keep his dick in his pants so why would she marry someone who couldn't stay faithful? Instead of telling her that she shouldn't, I encouraged her to follow her heart and to do what she felt was right. I guess she didn't want to have a child out of wedlock because they had a small but elaborate wedding at the Christiana Hilton. She was five months pregnant and honeymooned for two-weeks in France…a honeymoon that she paid for.

She rolled her eyes and looked away, "My marriage is going fine Brynn, did you check out the sells for this month? They've increased 10% since last month we're making a killing right now."

I already knew that my company was thriving but what I didn't know was how my best friend was really doing and I could tell by the change of subject that shit wasn't going like she wanted it to.

I looked at Lil's beautiful face and wondered why she settled for less when she didn't have to. Lilith was chocolate with light brown eyes and a warm smile. She had thick long hair that she kept in a ponytail and had a body to die for, but never wore revealing clothes to show it off. I didn't know if Hov forbid her from wearing provocative clothing or not. When we were teenagers she loved to show off her fat ass and large breasts, now everything she wore was high quality, yet too conservative for my taste. She wore shit from Talbot and Ann Taylor she dressed like an old mom when she's only twenty-five. Ever since she married the nigga I noticed a huge change in her and I didn't like it, but trying to be the best friend she was to me I kept my yap closed but I didn't know how long I would be able to.

"Would you like a cup of coffee Brynn?"

This girl knew damn well I didn't drink coffee.

"No but I'll take some Kailua and milk if you have it."

She frowned her face up, "Brynn you know I don't drink alcohol."

"Just like you know I don't drink coffee, Lil what's going on with you? Do I need to kick Hov's ass because you know I will." I was overprotective when it came to my best friend and I only wanted the best for her.

"No girl why are you tripping? Look I need to go pick them up from his mother's house call me later."

"Where the hell is his car at Lil? I just got here I want to spend some time with you."

"You've been here for over an hour and you daydreamed most of the time so hush, Brynn I really need to go." She escorted me to the door and kissed my cheek. I told her I loved her and to call me if she needed me but all she did was shut the door in my face. Now I had two things on my mind, sex and what's really going on with my best-friend.

Chapter 4

I went back to my townhouse changed and headed back out to hit the gym. Lilith's funny behavior had me pissed and my lack of a human sex was bothering me too. I arrived to the gym, surprisingly it wasn't crowded. I was relieved. I went inside and noticed there was nothing but a bunch of old moms walking on the treadmill. My mood was funky conversing with the old moms was the look for the day. *Weights it is…* I sat my towel down on the bench as I selected my playlist on my phone. A few moments later an aroma I knew all too well stole my attention. Like a wolf I sniffed out my prey. *Versace…*I only knew one person who wore that and his ass was in Jersey. I turned to the left and my heart skipped several beats. Our eyes met. In my mind I knew I should break the gaze. I didn't want to look thirsty. The body was saying something different. He walked over towards my direction. I was stuck. I was face to face with Mr. Sexy, himself, Emilio.

"Let me guess you're following me now?" Emilio asked staring into my eyes. His voice was just as sexy as he was, and it kind of reminded me of rapper Rick Ross's voice.

"Please don't flatter yourself Sir, by the way where's your wife?" I just had to ask because this man was so fucking fine that he made me nervous.

He laughed at my sarcasm, "She could be anywhere in the world right now, but why does that matter when you have my attention?" he said then flashed his million-dollar smile.

I bit down on my bottom lip, hoping that my pussy didn't open up and flood my panties. This nigga was Lance Gross sexy, I'm talking finer than Morris Chestnut and Denzel Washington put together. He had smooth bronze skin, with pink luscious lips, dimples in the corner of his mouth, pretty white teeth with pretty brown eyes, and I couldn't tell if he was Hispanic or Black. He was so fucking fine that I didn't even care what he was, in my head he was a mutt anyhow. He stood about 6'2 with a body like Dewayne 'The Rock' Johnson. His hair was in an abundance of black curls and his edge up was so precise, that it could only have been done with a straight razor.

"What's wrong? Cat got your tongue mommy?" he teased licking his lips. I wanted to so badly grab this nigga by the collar and ram my pussy on his face and I knew he could tell what I was thinking because my hard nipples and facial expression said it all. He reached out his hand to help me off the bench. I hesitated. He took hold of me and roughly pulled me towards him. *Aggressive...I like that.*

His breath was cool smelling like fresh mint leaves.

"I want you to take a ride with me." He licked lips.

Damn this dude is fine.

"I-I don't know Umm-I mean..." he had me tongue tied. I couldn't form a sentence.

"Shhh-just grab your bag and come with me. I'll bring you back to your car. I promise." Honestly I didn't care where we went, at that moment I just wanted to be with him.

We rode in silence to the unknown location. So many thoughts were going through my head. I was so out of pocket-married men were off limits. This was the reason I didn't believe in that shit. We arrived at our destination. The house was lovely. This had to be his home he shared with Onnie.

"Take off your clothes," he demanded as he stripped off his own.

I looked around and we were in the damn foyer. I know this nigga didn't think I was going to lay my ass on this floor. The wood was lovely but this was a bit much.

"Take off your clothes..." He stated while pulling his shirt over his head. He was impatient and in one swift move he snatched my shirt off of me. "You

29

don't know how to follow directions so I'll help you with that."

Instead of responding I let him unsnapped my bra and removed my spandex shorts along with my now drenched panties. He lustfully stared me up and down. I didn't know if this nigga was going to rape me or what either way I was down with it. Can rape be consensual?

"I've wanted you since the first time I saw you baby, I just didn't know how to approach you." he confessed. "I want to feel the warmth of your pussy, I want to taste you." He sounded like one of those lager commercials. He was definitely on his James Bond shit. He then walked over to me and lifted me up in his arms. He carried me up the elegant double stair case to this enormous bedroom. He gently laid me down on the California sized bed, and flipped me over on all fours so my ass was in the air. He licked my ass hole with rapid speed and bit down on my ass cheeks driving his thick long tongue inside my awaiting juice box as it dripped down on the sheets. My body temperature was hotter than the Hades and my fluids were running freely. He slowly sucked on my clitoris until it was swollen and used his fingers to unfold my secrets and licked between them until I begged him to stop. This nigga's tongue game was phenomenal; I had already came three times and was about to explode for the fourth time when he slowly slid inside my tight, wet walls. His big dick stretched my pussy out like a rubber band but it felt so good and relaxing that all I could do is moan.

"Oh shit, baby, goddamn!" I moaned through clenched teeth. I never expected it to be this good, and I can't ever remember coming like this either. He never said a word as he pounded away in my vice grip like pussy, but I knew he was enjoying himself by the plethora of fuck- faces he was making. I contracted my pussy muscles on his dick and arched my back, I was nearing an orgasm but I didn't have to tell him that because he could feel it.

"Cum all over my dick baby, make it rain girl!" my ass cheeks clapped and he stroked me harder and harder until I let out an ear piercing scream, and his dick was saturated in my love-potion. This nigga was filthy and I loved it!

Chapter 5

The sex -escapade between Emilio and I completely blew my mind, and for a few days I was stuck on stupid but then I realized that what we did was wrong, we could never be more than distant strangers. What else were we? I didn't even know the man and I let him run up in me unprotected like a misguided dumb-ass little girl. I went to the gym daily for two weeks hoping to bump into him. It didn't happen. Two weeks turned into three months and I hadn't seen him. Instead of dwelling on the bullshit, I threw myself into work and tried like hell to figure out what was really going on with Lilith. She barely said more than two words to me. My cousin had hooked up with some new Trinidadian guy whom she swore up and down was that 'nigga' and never wanted to leave his side, so I wasn't talking to her much nowadays either. I spent my days alone or doing research on my competition. My parents called me continuously, asking me if I'd met the one yet and my answer always remained the same; I'm not looking for the one and the love of my life will forever be MONEY. This year I was trying to bring in the BIG bucks and I had a lot of things to do, yearning over a married man wasn't one of them.

"Brynn I'm telling you this nigga is the real mu-fucking deal you gots to meet one of his boys, I'm telling you they all caked up."
Since arriving at the Caribbean Cafe this hoe hadn't shut her mouth. I could tell that whoever this nigga was had her nose wide open; as usual, and sad to say but Pam was a sucker for a big dick and a smile.

"Now you already know that I am not checking for no nigga right now all my focus is on money, hell I even cut Shock off the other day because he kept trying to smother me and shit." I confessed feeling slightly aggravated by the thought of him smothering me.

"You cut Shock off? Why? That nigga is too fucking sexy to be cut loose." She paused for a moment. "Well shit since you did pass me that number I got some tricks for his ass!"

I didn't know if Pam was dead-ass serious or just joking and I honestly didn't want to find out. "Bitch I'm just fucking with you but if you wasn't my cousin I'd be on it! Come to my place tonight around eight for a few drinks. I gotta go but here's my half of the check."

She handed me a fifty-dollar bill and left. I continued to eat my food and wondered if I would be making the right decision by going to her house.

I pulled up in front of Pam's condo and saw a pearl Aston Martin Vanquish One-77 parked next to a Red Porsche 911. I knew that Pam was telling nothing short of the truth when she said this dude and his friends were caked up. I was now up to the challenge; bitches may not like me but I didn't care because only money excites me. Yes, I had my own money, but why die trying to spend my shit when I can die trying to spend their shit? My point exactly, besides I needed something to get my mind off Emilio, because truth be told he had me wide open literally without my permission. I rang Pam's doorbell and gladly anticipated the unknown I was ready for anything, anything to get my mind off that nigga.

"Damn bitch you're here on time tonight? You must have been really beat huh?" I couldn't contain my laughter because I knew she was right. I usually arrived everywhere fashionably late.

"Yeah well you know people change but um where he at?"

"Oh they left out for a second but girl you look cute when you cop those?" she asked referring to my new silver YSL heels.

"Oh I bought these last weeks and to think they were the last pair!" I said sticking my tongue out at her. My cousin had a touch of the e-virus. Envy.

Anything I would buy she went out and copped after me. Usually I'd agree that imitation is a form of flattery, but Pam took shit to the next level sometimes. I could see her now formulating a plan to go out and buy a pair on the sly. I was wearing the hell out of a pewter Emilio Pucci jumper that made my ass appear even fatter than it was and my hair was fried and laid to the side to perfection thanks to the Dominicans on Second Street. It was times like this when I enjoyed my ethnicity. My hair wasn't thick but it wasn't thin either which made it easier for me to manage.

"How they leave out for a second when both cars are parked out front?" I interrupted her minuscule thought process.

"Bitch how you know they're not my neighbors' cars?"

"Bitch, they ain't got parking stickers on them and they're not in the parking the garage. You know security does not play." I retorted. "White people don't leave shit out their like that on display. They know better. That's some show boat nigga shit."

"Oh well, they rode bikes that's how and don't ask me who the surprise guest is because Alex didn't tell me his name or nothing, he didn't even come in Alex met him outside." Fuck the cars out front, if Pam didn't see the nigga for all I know he could look like Danny Glover and that's ugly. My stomach churned thinking about it.

"I don't think this is a good idea Pam I'm about to go home girl you telling me you haven't seen the nigga either?" I stressed. I walked towards the door when two men stepped inside.

"Damn leaving so soon? I heard a familiar voice ask. I looked up and was standing face to face with the boogie man himself; Emilio.

"Ay baby this is my mans Emilio, Emilio this my baby Pam, and her cousin ahh what's your name again ma?"

Looking Emilio dead in the eye I said, "Brynn, my name is Brynn its nice meeting you Alex I was just on my way out." I pushed past Emilio and Alex. I practically ran to my car. I heard Pam calling out my name but I ignored her ass and kept moving. This shit was too ironic. This was the devil. I couldn't believe that I spent all this time trying to get him off my mind just to run into the nigga anyway. Was this a coincident or was me and Emilio meant to be somehow? I didn't take the time to find out because I took my scary ass home. I'd deal with Pam's ass later.

The next day I went to Christiana Mall to do a little shopping. Usually I'd bring Pam along with me but I knew she was still mad about the way I left the night before. I was leaving Armani Exchange with three bags full of clothes when I saw Onnie Emilio's wife walking in looking dazzling in an asymmetrical black Valentino dress, Fred Leighton gems, and a black pair of Christian Louboutin pumps. Her long hair was swept up in an up do and her make-up was alright. The blush on her cheeks appeared more like bruises. I don't know where she got her blending technique but she needed to try again because that was a fail; and who wears all that to the mall is all I was thinking? We made eye contact for a brief minute before she finally said something.

"Hey aren't you Mina's friend? Uhh, Brynn right?"

She knew damn well she remembered my name. I was at her restaurant at least three times a month.

"Yup Mina's my girl. How are you Onnie?"

Onnie didn't answer me right away because she was too busy checking out my attire, lucky for me I always stayed fresh. Today I was rocking a tight blue Marc Jacobs jeans with a low cut lily white blouse with a pair of five inch Alexander McQueen pumps. My hair was in a sloppy but sleek French braid and a hint of blush, *applied correctly* and lip-gloss completed my look. I didn't need a cocktail dress and six inch heels to shop at a basic mall. I was fly yet comfortable.

"Oh, I am *great* sweetheart, check this out, my husband just bought me a brand new tennis bracelet." She held up her wrist so I can see that ice that damn near gave me cataracts. I felt myself getting jealous and I wanted to get out of there quick but she continued to brag about her husband, my old fuck buddy.

"Girl he is so good to me, he keeps a big smile on my face it feels so good loving somebody, when somebody loves you back. Are you single Brynn?"

I looked at her like she was crazy I don't even know her like that and she questioning me. She was corny as hell with that line from that old ass song. I wanted so bad to say I know what you mean. I fucked your husband in your bed bitch. I knew that would turn into a situation and I wasn't about drama, especially with a nigga's wife.

"Oh that's cute. Single I am, but not at all lonely. I got to get going girl I'll see you around Onnie." I said before stepping off.

She reached out and touched my hand and said "I'm sure you will," and walked inside the store. The look in her eyes made me think she knew something. I know it was my conscience because no one knew what Emilio and I did.

I was just pulling up in front of my house when I saw a Platinum Porsche Panorama parked in front of my house. I didn't recognize the car and truth be told I wasn't trying to all I wanted to do was take a shower and catch up on 'Pretty Little Liars'. I loved that show and I already missed two episodes. I grabbed my bags out the trunk and unlocked my front door. I took my first step in the door when I felt a hand grab me. I jumped out my skin and screamed, but before I could say another word. My mouth was covered by a large hand and I felt my body being

38

lifted in the air. Oh shit! I'm about to die at the age of twenty-five! Oh shit.

I was thrown on my bed and my clothes were ripped off my body. I didn't know who my abductor was because he was dressed in all black with a ski mask concealing his identity.

"What the fuck do you want from me? I have about three thousand in cash and some credit cards take it all just don't kill me!" I was terrified; I knew I should have moved to a gated community. I thought I was safe but now I knew I was wrong. *I should have moved down Middletown or in Kent County some damn where next to my parents like they suggested.* I felt my abductor pulling my panties past my ankles and then I realized that I was about get raped. "Please don't rape me please just take the money and go!" I felt a soft tongue slide against my clitoris and a moan escaped my mouth. *Why the fuck am I moaning when I'm about to get raped...* I wondered but I couldn't help it. His tongue felt so familiar and I closed my eyes in anticipation. He was eating the shit out my pussy and I was coming like it was going out of style. I was still somewhat scared but the sensation was too good to deny. I closed my eyes and held his head tight as I came on his face.

"Oh shit that felt so good damn it!" I screamed.

"I'm glad you enjoyed it baby, now it's time for you to enjoy this dick." The man removed his mask and I got the shock of my life I saw Emilio's sexy face and juicy lips. This nigga was insane. I wanted to run and hide, I wanted to make him leave and tell him to never come back because he just assaulted my pussy with his tongue but instead I pushed him back on the bed and mounted him. His dick quickly filled my walls and I felt an electric current shoot through my body. I rode him up and down, round and round until I could no longer. I looked into his sexy face as I came long and hard, it was then that I knew that I was in deep shit. I had feelings for this man and I never saw it coming. His gray eyes had me going and his luscious lips begged me to kiss them and I did. We kissed passionately while he was still inside of me and I swear when he grabbed my hair and forced his tongue down my throat I squirted all over him. I mean literally, my pussy was leaking like a running faucet from a kiss alone, which never happened to me before, ever.

"Damn baby it's like that?" Emilio asked as he felt my candy rain drip down his dick and upper torso.

"Yeah baby it's like that cuz you got it like that." I said as I laid my head on his chest and fell asleep. The sun was rising when I awoke to Emilio standing over me smiling. He was draped in a white towel and water dripped from his body.

"I figured you wouldn't mind if I took a shower how are you feeling baby?" I had to be dreaming, there was no way that this fine ass married nigga was in my house standing over me looking like lunch meat. His body was chiseled and muscular and his body was marked up like a subway in Philly.

"No baby I don't mind don't you think you should be getting home to the wife?" I asked. He laughed and went back in my walk in bathroom to brush his teeth. I needed to slap myself. I was calling this nigga baby and he broke into my house. He came back into the room and sat down beside me on my bed.

"You got me tripping boo but I just had to have you." He removed the covers from my body like he was looking for imperfections. I suddenly felt self-conscious. "No baby, don't do that don't feel insecure, you're perfect." It was like he could read my mind. I didn't know what to feel or think. "I love you." he said and I just knew that I had to be hearing things.

"You what? You love me how? You don't even know me." I sat up and grabbed the covers. Now he was insulting my intelligence. I wasn't one of those dick dizzy chicks that could fall for the bull. "You fuck me and disappear for three months-break in my house and take the pussy again-now you love me? That's some fuck shit. You don't even know me!"

"I said I love you Brynn, and I know you well enough to know that I love you."

Was this man out of his mind or was he serious? He just sat here and told me he loved me and he didn't even know my last name. I knew I had feelings for him too-lust! I'm not sure if its love. *Wait a minute...feelings...not sure if it's love? Chill Brynn...* I checked my thoughts.

"I can see that you're overwhelmed but that's cool ma, I'm going to head on out. I'm not going anywhere. You're mine." I watched as he slipped back on his clothes and he gave me a kiss on the lips. "We just sealed our relation." He walked out the door leaving me naked and dumbfounded.

What the fuck? I looked over at my clock and saw that it was only 6 a.m. I forced myself to sleep for a couple of hours. When I woke up I went downstairs into the kitchen to find a stack of money on the counter and three red velvet boxes which I knew right away was jewelry. I didn't bother opening the jewelry boxes but I grabbed the cash and counted out five thousand dollars. I didn't know what kind of shit this nigga was on but I was down to play. If he didn't give a fuck about his wife why should I? He came to me not the other way around so why feel guilty when he damn sure wasn't? I hopped in the shower. I had a mental debate with myself. I knew this shit was wrong but his dick was right. Messing with a married man was a dangerous game...His dick game was wicked and his money was long-I would be a fool not to play.

Chapter 6

It's been two months since that day Emilio confessed to loving me and my life changed drastically. He was staying at my house at least three days a week and the days that we didn't spend at my house we spent at the Embassy Suites or the Hilton. He bought me so much jewelry that I started to feel like a rapper from down south. I rarely spent my own money nowadays and Lilith seemed to be happy too. Maybe she and Hov worked whatever problems they were having out because home girl smiled now more than she did in the past year. Pam was still hanging in tough with Alex and we sometimes double dated. I quickly learned that he and Emilio were business partners and known each other since P.S 192. They were both immigrants; Emilio from the Dominican Republic, and Alex was from Trinidad. Alex was deported a few years back and somehow he made it back to the states. They grew up in New York but moved to Delaware when their business expanded.

When I asked Emilio what was exactly his business he kissed my forehead and told me that he worked in construction which I knew was a lie, he was too fly and suave to be getting his hands dirty. Even Alex's pretty ass dressed like a don. Every day they dressed in business attire, which by the way was either tailor made or Armani and the designer shoes they wore were not fit for construction work. I wanted to pry more about his business but I got too caught up in the dick to bother. He was everything I wanted in a man; he was paid, hardworking, loving, caring, and respectful. He always complimented me and made me feel special and throughout everything he had my back. He was such an intellectual man; he even gave me pointers from a business aspect. He too owned a few businesses, and knew what it was like to be a boss. The fact that he was married no longer bothered me because that was a part of him that I didn't deal with. As far as I was concerned he was my man, and her husband. Whenever I called he answered and whatever I asked for he provided it no questions asked. By now I was head over heels in love with him and everyone around me knew it.

My parents wanted to meet the man that kept a smile on my face but I wasn't ready for all that because technically he wasn't mine and I knew my parents would be very disappointed in me if they found out he was married. They were two seconds from becoming Jesus himself so the bible would have went upside my head and they would have tried their best to have me in the Pastors office for counseling sessions.

"I am so hungry let's hit up 'Onnie's Place'," Pam said on our way home from the Natural Hair Expo that was held at the Double Tree Hotel. I had a booth set up there every year. I usually wouldn't go. This year I wanted to check out the market to see if there was anything for me to be concerned about. I was good. The line for my booth wrapped around the conference room.

I shot her the gas face and she sucked her teeth.

"I forgot you was fucking her husband how is the dick anyway with his mutt ass?" I couldn't help but to laugh because indeed my boo was a mutt. His mother was Dominican and I later learned his father was Italian. I knew drugs had to be in the mix somewhere because that match was rare. When they came to the states he was raised by his Spanish grandmother because his parents were drug addicts. He said his father, Anthony had a bad blow habit and that his mother Marie was addicted to pain killers. He never talked much about his family though, but he always referred to Alex as his brother.

"Don't be calling my baby a mutt and the dick is trash!" I said to throw Pam off, cousin or no cousin she was a hoe and I knew she had a little thing for Emilio even after she knew he was off limits. One thing about Pam was no matter how much money a nigga had if his dick was small she wouldn't be bothered with him. She said money and a big dick went hand in hand like a baton. "But his head is great so I keep him around." She shot me a sly look and rolled her eyes.

"Bitch I know your ass is lying to keep my ass from him but it's all good, Alex is all I need, the nigga threatened to kill me if I gave his pussy away so you're good for now but can we please go to 'Onnie's Place' I've been wanting some curry goat for a minute now, please Brynn I promise we don't have to sit down and eat we can just order to go." After listening to her beg for twenty minutes I finally gave in but told her that I wasn't about to eat at the restaurant knowing that I was nailing her husband. What if the bitch tries to poison me? I'd be a fool to eat there. Pam didn't care all she wanted was some curry goat, rice and peas. I drove in silence hoping that there wouldn't be any drama when we got there.

When we walked inside the first person I saw was Emilio. He and Onnie were sitting at a table enjoying a nice meal and also what appeared to be each other's company. I wasn't even angry until I saw Onnie kiss Emilio on the lips.

"Damn Brynn your nigga's a pimp!" Pam said not making me feel any better. I wanted to go over there and whip his ass but instead I calmed myself down and told Pam to hurry up and order her food so we can go. I stood back in the corner so I wouldn't be seen but Onnie spotted me anyway and called me over to her table.

"Hey Brynn girl come here how are you?" she was stunning as usual in a tight blue Stella McCartney sheath and a hot pair of Giuseppe pumps. Her hair; which had added tracks was pulled in a sophisticated bun and her make-up was flawless. I could tell Emilio was a little shocked to see me but his cool ass played it off like the suave nigga he was and smiled at me and said hello as if he wasn't sucking the crème filling out my pussy the night before.

"Hello Mr. Fuentes enjoying a nice evening with the wife? How cute…"

"Yes girl it is because since he's been working on a new project lately we haven't spent any time together. I've been missing my husband like you wouldn't believe, Brynn are you still single?"

Little did she know, I was that *project*.

I observed Emilio with a devilish smile, "Yes I am Onnie girl why do you ask? You have somebody for me?" I knew this would have Emilio squirming in his seat.

She smiled modestly, "Actually I do, my brother Nash is newly single and ready to mingle. He asked me if I knew of any single ladies and I thought of you." I let out a light chuckle and I could hear Emilio clearing his throat.

"Sounds like a plan I would love to meet your brother is he here?" I said turning my head like I was searching for him. I knew this would piss him off even more. That was my goal.

Onnie laughed and tapped Emilio on the shoulder.

"Baby, don't you think she and Nash would make a cute couple?" Emilio looked at me closely and excused himself from the table; he said he had a phone call to make suddenly.

Onnie asked me to sit in his seat as she talked about her brother Nash and his job as a Pilot in the Unites States Air force. She showed me a few pictures of him and I had to admit he was a cutie with pretty curly hair and a mocha complexion. I was about to ask her where Nash was, however, my phone vibrated in my cream clutch interrupting me. It was a message from Emilio demanding for me to meet him in the men's room. I ignored the message and continued my conversation with Onnie as if we were long lost friends. My phone went off two more times before I excused myself and went to the bathroom to see what he wanted. I passed Pam on the way there and told her to sit tight and that I would be right back. As soon as I stepped foot in the Men's room Emilio grabbed my neck and stuck his tongue down my throat. He ran his fingers through my already wild hair and licked my collar bone.

"If you give my pussy away I'll fucking kill you Brynn." He picked me up and sat me down on the sink and assaulted my neck and face with kisses. "You're mine." he whispered in my ear and dipped his fingers in my wetness. He pulled up my skirt and pushed my panties aside and roughly entered me. His big dick felt so good in my tightness that I closed my eyes and savored each stroke. Here we were in his wife's restaurant fucking. He didn't have a care in the world and neither did I, he was hitting me with the death strokes and I was throwing the pussy back at him like we were playing basketball and we were on the same team.

"I fucking love you!" I whimpered as he feverishly pumped deep inside of my tunnel. He placed his hand over my mouth and fucked me harder. He looked me dead in the eyes and mouthed he loved me too. He placed his hands around my neck and I felt my heart beat speed up. He was softly choking me and cutting off my air supply but it made my already wet pussy wetter and I came all over the sink. He let out a loud grunt and released his babies inside my canal. I love that shit. I didn't even complain I just kissed him passionately and left him with his pants down in the Men's room.

"Damn bitch! What the fuck were you doing in the bathroom that long?" Instead of me driving her back home she was staying at my place for the night so I had to put up with her nosy ass.

"I was doing me." I smiled but my rosy cheeks gave me away and she knew what was up.

"No you didn't fuck that man in the bathroom of his *wife's* restaurant? And they call me a hoe bitch! You are officially a scandalous hoe. You on some dizzy shit." She said with all seriousness.

I laughed at my cousin but said nothing more on the subject, I was never the type to fuck and tell anyway. Dizzy, please I wasn't doing dumb shit for the dick. I was in complete control of the situation. I wasn't under any type of spell. When I started to act irrational then she could call me dizzy. Right now I was enjoying myself. I'd leave her nosy ass in suspense. When we pulled up in front of my house I saw Alex sitting on his Kawasaki smoking a blunt.

"Bout time yawl got here I've been sitting out here for almost an hour." Pam got out the car and hugged and kissed him. I knew my cousin was in love for real this time because she was never into PDA and here she was hugging and kissing on Alex with no shame.

"Awe don't be jealous Brynn my brother is on his way don't worry ma-ma." Alex always had something funny to say and this time was no different.

"Uh ah baby we just saw him at the restaurant and they had a little rendezvous in the bathroom, she's aight." Pam and her big ass mouth why did that bitch go and say that and have my cheeks flushed again.

"Damn my brother got you like that?" he asked handing Pam a helmet.

"No, I have your brother like that- he's married but just not to his wife." I snickered and gave him a hug and kiss on the cheek.

"I heard that, ma. You're sealed that's stronger than that paper shit anyway." He said and the three of us laughed. Pam got on the back of his bike and put her helmet on. "You can't be the only one getting some dick, I'll spend the night with you next time but this time I need a sexual healing, love you!"

"I love you too Pam, Alex take care of my cousin bye."

After they pulled off I walked into my house and showered. I logged on Facebook and saw that I had a friend request from a guy name 'Nash Torres' and I knew right away it was Onnie's brother. She doesn't waste any time does she? Instead of accepting the request I logged off and went to bed. I was so damn tired that I didn't even bother putting on pajamas; I just lay on my bed and went to sleep.

Chapter 7

"So mommy tells me that you have a new man in your life when are you going to bring him around so we can meet him?" my sister Amelie asked me as I took a seat at the kitchen table next to her. My sister looked just like my mother, but had a take charge attitude like my father. She graduated from Rutgers with a degree in nursing a few years ago but she never put that degree to use because she got married and started having kids. I never understood her logic in having kids because I damn sure didn't want any but I loved my niece and nephew dearly. Her oldest, my nephew, Cameron was the cutest little boy ever with black curly hair and pretty brown eyes like his father. He was three years-old and bad as hell but my sister insisted on having another child. My niece Ciara was only about three months old and cried most of the time. She was cute but that crying shit blew me I kissed my nephew Cameron in the face a dozen times before I answered her question.

"Amelie honestly I don't know when I will bring him over we're still kind of new." I put Cameron down on the floor and let him go so he can he finish watching cartoons.

"Mommy says you're in love is that true? I'm amazed that you are capable of loving something other than yourself and money?"

I looked at Amelie and laughed.

"I wouldn't say love, I care about him deeply. All of that doesn't matter all I know is that right now I'm happy Amelie." I sighed giving her the signal that I didn't want to talk about it anymore but she continued.

"I just think that maybe you should bring him over for dinner so we can meet him and stuff, maybe he will marry you and have babies. I looked at my sister and wondered what type of pills she was snorting.

"Amelie how many times do I have to tell you that I don't want kids, and that being an Aunty is enough for me? And who the hell said anything about marriage? All men cheat! Why would I bother with that? Ugh, Amelie I don't know what fantasy world you live in but I don't live there with you, you're alone sis sorry to break it to you." My mother walked in holding baby Ciara and I was already working on my exit.

"Don't stop talking on my behalf ladies, but Brynn your sister is right you should bring him over for dinner I would love to meet him." I knew she was serious.

"Mom, when I find out which direction we're going in I'll bring him over to meet you but until than uh-ah." I kissed my mother's cheek and told her and my sister I'd see them later because I knew if I didn't leave we'd spend all day talking about how I needed to settle down.

***

My doorbell rang the next morning around ten in the morning, right after Emilio and I just finished having some mind blowing sex. I put on my robe and walked down the stairs to see who the hell was at my house ringing my bell so early. When I looked out the peephole and saw my mother and sister standing outside my door I panicked. What the fuck were they doing here? I opened the door and smiled.

"Hola, Senora, Como estas?" I said to my mother in Spanish, I asked her how she was doing but I really wanted to ask her why the fuck she was here so early.

"Bueno, bebe y tu?" She replied pushing past me and walking inside my house like I invited her in. My sister followed behind her and I closed the front door and followed them into the kitchen where my mother was messing with the coffee maker.

"Como estas la hermana?" my sister finally said checking out my kitchen.

Cut the shit Amelie, why did you bring mommy here?" I knew it had to be her idea to come over my house. Amelie was nosy like that, if you didn't tell her what she wanted to know she went snooping for the answers.

"What's the problem Brynn mommy's not allowed over your house? What's up with the Spanish? Are you denying your nationality again?" I sucked my teeth, "No one said she couldn't come...I just want to know why! I can ask why! It's my house, right?" I asked my mother.

"I wanted to meet this mystery man of yours, of course Brynn your sister said we should just drive over here so we can catch him before he leaves." I shot Amelie a look to let her know I was going to get on her ass later about this.

"Hey Brynn baby I'm going to put these dirty sheets in the wash and head out okay baby?" Emilio came into the kitchen dressed in a tank-top showcasing his muscles and tight build, and a pair of True Religion jeans and the new 12's. He had his hair cut the day before, today he was looking like a straight up Dominican rather than an Italian like he usually looked. Emilio was the sexiest man I've ever met; I couldn't help to drool over him as he stood in my face smelling like heaven. Emilio looked at my mother and sister and then back at me.

"Hello my name is Emilio, I'm Brynn's fiancé you must be her mother, Nisa and sister Amelie?" Fiancé?

Now he was doing the most! I had to take a look at my left hand to make sure he ain't slipped any diamonds on it while I was sleep. It was empty. I never told him my mother or sister's name so I was shocked that he knew who they were as well.

My mother eyed Emilio up and down and smiled. I knew she thought my baby was fine and I couldn't help but to smile myself.

"Yes, I am Brynn's mother Nisa and you can call me Miss Nisa." My mother openly flirted with my man. I laughed and so did Emilio. She then turned in my direction. "Is there something you need to tell me?" There was a twinkle of excitement in her. Too bad I was about to put a dimmer on things. I wasn't nobody's fiancé. It wasn't possible-he was already married.

"There's nothing to tell mother. I'm not engaged. Emilio plays a lot of games." I said eyeing him.
He smiled playfully and turned his attention back to my mother. I could tell that he thought my mother was sexy because every man with eyes thought the same thing. My mother didn't look a day over thirty and was wearing the hell out of a pair of Seven Jeans and a flirty Donna Karan blouse with four inch heels. Her hair was curly and smelled of fresh roses; my mother was still the shit at forty-seven. Amelie was still giving him the once over but I didn't care because my mother approved of him so fuck what she thought.

"Nice meeting you ladies but I got to go, babe I'm taking your car is that okay?"

"Oh yeah, sure baby my keys are on the mantle." He went into the back room and started the washing machine. He came back and kissed me deeply before he left and my sister was taking it all in.

"So he drives your car and you claim that it's not serious." Amelie said to me after she heard Emilio pull off. We were now sitting in my plush living room; my mother and sister were drinking coffee while I drank tea. "Well it's not, and it's only a car Amelie what's the deal who cares?" I said sipping my tea.

"I care, does he have his own car or is he a bum?" I looked at Amelie and laughed, "Only you date the bums and yes his car is in the garage, thank you." my sister was getting on my nerves and I was ready for her to leave.

"He's handsome Brynn, is he Latin? Is this why you were speaking Spanish?" my mother asked giving Amelie a funny look. "Um his mother is Dominican and his father is Italian."

"Oh so he speaks Spanish?"

I sighed, "Yes a little mother why? If he didn't would that be a problem?"

"No Brynn I am just asking don't get offended child. Does he know you are *not* Spanish? I know the little games you play with your looks. Does he know French is your native tongue?"

Native tongue? I'm from America and I speak English. My mother was irritating me. She was referring to a situation that happened with a guy name Javier Lopez. He was an exception from my street nigga addiction. I cheated on him but he was something special. The issue we had was that his parents only allowed him to date Spanish girls and I loved him to death. We were seventeen and we were a couple until I was twenty. He had never met my father only my mother because she could pass for Spanish. Well, good ole Javier was about to pop the question and believe it or not I was going to say yes to the damn dress! He planned a dinner at his parents' house. He invited my mother and of course she bought the whole family including my *African American* father. That night Javier and his parents found out I was a fraud with a capital F and he cut me off like Delmarva Power. I was so pissed because I purchased Rosetta Stone to learn Spanish. I even gave my mother a few lessons. I would have told him the truth after I said I do. It would have been too late to leave me then.

"I think he's a nice catch for you, when are you going to marry him?"

I spat out my tea, "Mommy who said anything about marriage? We just started dating."

"Yeah, mommy she's right and he's probably already married." Amelie said rolling her eyes at me and sipping her coffee.

"Amelie what is your fucking problem?" I sat my cup down and stepped to her.

"Nothing Brynn, I just think he's a thug that's all, a little ghetto too."

"How in the hell could you think that when he only said a few words to you? You're dumb."

"Children that's enough." My mother interjected stopping what was going to be a full-fledge fight between two sisters. My mother stood up and told Amelie that she was ready to go to the mall. Amelie went outside and waited for my mother in the car because she claimed that I was shooting her daggers. My mother gave me a hug and whispered in my ear, "she's just jealous Brynn, I love you." I kissed my mother on the cheek and told her to call me when she got home. I closed and locked the door behind her and laughed. Amelie was seriously ego tripping and showing her ass my mother was right, she was jealous. I called up Pam to tell her what went down and she laughed.

"You know Amelie has always been jealous of you with her corny ass," she said. We hung up with plans to meet up later.

Chapter 8

When I met up with Pam at the Red Lobster I almost didn't recognize her. She had a short 1990's Toni Braxton haircut dyed honey blonde, which was unusual because she usually wore long weaves. She was dressed elegantly in a black Chanel skirt with the matching bag and pumps. "Damn did somebody pull a Cher and Dion in here?' I asked her referring to the movie 'Clueless'.

"Yeah girl, Alex wants me to go au natural and this was the closest he'll ever see me natural. I don't got hair like you my shit thick; I need my perms so I just got it cut short. You like it?"

I looked at her new doo and smiled, "Yeah its fly cousin real fly... on you." I joked not really feeling her new look. I really didn't understand why she was changing herself for a nigga. I wouldn't tell her that. Pam was the type that took shit too personal and would run home crying about it. She waited for my approval so I approved. "It's nice, where you get it done at?" "I went to Mia...remember Mia from Brookmont? "Oh yeah she did a good ass job, come on lets go sit at the bar I need a drink or two."

Pam and I ended up getting drunk as skunks at the bar and were yelling all types of obscenities at the air when a pretty brown skin chick with a small cute shape took a seat next to us. Pam gave her the once over and tapped me, "What Pam?" I snapped so ready to go. The Margarita's had caught up to me and I wanted nothing more than to go home. I had two missed calls from Emilio and I knew he would be pissed when I finally answered.

"Shut up cow isn't that Felito walking in the door?" Felito was my sister's husband and baby daddy of four years, I looked up to see if my sister was behind him but she wasn't. I was about to call out to him when I noticed the chick who was just sitting next to me was now in Felito's face hugging and kissing on him.

"Oh shit!" Pam said in a drunken stupor. I was just as shocked not that he was cheating but who he was cheating with. She was total opposite of my sister. She was short, thick with a ghetto booty! She looked like she was fresh off the DART bus. There was nothing wrong with riding buses but this bitch looked like the stroller with six crumb snatchers straggling along type. Aunt Ora was right; all men cheat. Hell, Emilio was cheating on his wife with me so the proof was in the pudding. Amelie walked around like her shit didn't stink; all the while she had a cheating ass husband now ain't that about a dumb bitch? I thought about my next move silently, suddenly I was sobering up. I knew that there was no way in hell that I was going to let his ass get away with playing my fucking sister. Fast on my feet, I grabbed my drink and walked over to him and poured it all over his curly head. The chick he was with started to pop fly and I mushed her ass and dared her to get loose. The crazed look in Felito's eyes let me know that he was ready to act weak but I was prepared for his tortilla eating ass. My mother always praised Amelie for marrying him but I never saw the greatness of it. I had nothing against it but my mother almost always forced us to date within our culture. I know she loved Spanish people, but shit Felito was a no good ass Nuyorican from the start. He hailed from Armaningo Ave, a drug infested area in North Philly.

"Bitch who the fuck is you?" the woman yelled and I laughed.

"Felito is married to my fucking sister bitch so that makes me his sister in law! Furthermore, I don't think my sister would appreciate you kissing all over her man!" Pam was mushing Felito repeatedly and a crowd was now forming. Whap! Felito had hauled off and smacked the shit out of me and it sent me flying to the floor.

"Nigga you done fucked up now!" Pam yelled as she jumped on his back and started trying to scratch his eyes out but he was simply too strong for her. The manager was now helping me up and had a concerned look on her face. She motioned for one of the employees to call the police and I knew shit was about to get ugly fast. I touched my nose and felt the blood and went the fuck off.

"Puta! Are you fucking loco?" I attacked Felito with all my might, the girl he was with had vanished and me and Pam was going to work on his ass. He finally flipped Pam off his back like she weighed 5 pounds and sent her crashing down on top of me. Felito was a big stocky dude standing a little over six feet and weighing 260 pounds. His usual tan face was now fire red and I could tell he wanted to stump the shit out of us but the police arrived

"What's going in here!" a Caucasian officer yelled pulling out his ghetto bracelets. "Who's going to jail?" he asked looking at me and then Pam and finally at Felito who was still steaming mad.

Just than a familiar voice shouted, "Everything's fine officer I'll take it from here." I don't know how but Emilio was standing there angry with Alex, dressed in nothing but cashmere sweats and a white beater with Timberland boots.

The officer looked at Emilio and smiled. "Emilio what's good my man?" the officer asked taking the bass out his voice. He shook Emilio and Alex's hand.

"Everything straight fam," Emilio said peering at me and looking at Felito like he wanted him dead. "How's my aunt doing?" he asked the officer and I now noticed the slight resemblance between the two. He must be Italian because I didn't detect any

Spanish features. "She's' fine, been asking about you man come by soon."

"Oh, I plan on it Joey I see you've met my girl, Brynn." He said through clenched teeth. "Brynn baby, this is my cousin Joey." As on cue, Joey asked me how I was doing and left. That was the strangest thing because I could have sworn that we all were about to go to jail. Officer Joey looked as if he was ready to pepper spray all of us and handcuff us but all that changed the moment Emilio walked in.

Pam spat on Felito and quickly ran into Alex's burly arms. Emilio walked over to me and examined the dry blood that was on my lips and nose and kissed me. "Go get in the car now you and Pam." Emilio spoke with so much malice that I didn't ask any questions. I left out with Pam on my heels.

***

Later on that night as I lay in the bed thinking about Emilio my house phone rang and from the caller ID I knew that it was my sister Amelie. "Hello"

"Brynn oh my god Felito is in the hospital he was found beaten on the side of the road! Oh my god why would someone do this to him?" she cried and I quickly sat up and turned on the lamp. The realization that Emilio was responsible for this shit hit me and I was starting to feel dizzy. "Okay just calm down what hospital are you at I'll come see you?"

"No, you can't see him like this I'll call you later, bye." My sister is fucking crazy; she's always worried about how something looks to other people and her reputation. My guess is she didn't want this to get back to his family or even worse our family, but hell by sunrise all that would be down the drain. I rolled over and tried my best to get some sleep but it was hard falling asleep especially when Emilio wasn't lying next to me.

Chapter 9

I was at my parents' house looking at a battered and bruised Felito, whom my sister was waiting on hand and foot like a baby and I couldn't help but to laugh. This nigga is a dirty dick dog and my sister didn't have the slightest clue. I tried to tell her on many occasions but she kept brushing me off like lint so I came up with a better idea; I was going to let the chick confront my sister about it. The chick whose name was Shar informed me that she knew nothing about Felito being married to my sister let alone having children with her. So basically the nigga was a good liar and pretender but I was going to expose his trifling ass! I knew she'd be hurt but oh well she needed to know the truth, the whole truth. I was going to tell her that Felito got his ass whipped because he put his hands on me and Pam and how we busted him kissing on Shar in Red Lobsters.

"Amelie, do you feel like riding with me to Target so I can pick up a few things?" I asked her hoping she'd agree. She looked over at Felito and then back at me.

"Felito needs me to stay here with him Brynn maybe some other time, besides you know I don't like going to that ghetto store."

"It wasn't ghetto when I bought Ciara's baby shower gifts from there was it? Just come with me please Amelie I don't ask you for much." I poked my bottom lip out. Felito shot her a glance that didn't go unnoticed but she decided to go with me anyway. Since the incident Felito never said more than two-words to me but what did I care? I didn't give a fuck about him, and from the ass whipping he got neither did Emilio. Emilio didn't come home the night of the beating, but the next day when he did I let his ass have it mainly for not coming home and secondly because I could. I asked him numerous questions about the incident but he refused to talk about it. All he said was that he handled it. He said that Felito's mouth said that he was a boss but his actions screamed soldier, damn I never looked at shit like that before. Felito did walk around like King Kong only to get laid out like Goliath. He owned his own recycling business, well his father owned the business but Felito and his brother Marco did majority of the work. When I first met him he somewhat reminded me of a straight Ricky Martin, no lie all that nigga did was dance around in circles and sing, off key might I add. But that was years ago, after a while I deemed him to be a lame, a loser, the sorry that nigga he is. The entire way to the store she complained and hollered about Felito's injuries like the softy she was. I received a text message from Shar on my Obama phone. I got that when I altered my tax returns so I could get Medicaid and some food stamps. Shit everybody did it. She said that she was already there waiting on me. Usually I would love a bitch that was on time but this bitch was not my type if Felito was what her type of dude. It had been a minute since I had dealt with a female sexually. Although the urge would pop up time to time, Emilio reminded me how much I appreciated an amazing dick down. I didn't care how big the strap on was there was nothing like a strong back and a fat long dick. All flesh no plastic. We pulled up in front of the Target at the mall twenty-five minutes later and already Amelie was complaining. "Oh Lord, Brynn please do not have me in here all day. You know my husband needs me right now, I hate this fucking ghetto ass store why couldn't we just go to the one on 202 or something?" I looked over at Amelie's dumb ass and immediately regretted bringing her ass here. By no means was she ready for what I was about to deliver but there was no turning back now. I got out of the car and grabbed my Michael Kors Hampton bag and checked my compact mirror. I was on point as usual. I wore this cute little settee I picked up from Sears; yes, *Sears* the Kardashian collection had some cute shit.

I looked over at my sister and frowned, why would she wear some dingy ass *that hoe over there* tights out in public. Regardless of what she had on my sister was cute but her gear was the worst. It's like when she got married T-shirts and tights were her uniform. That would irritate the hell out of me. Only hoes wore tights every day. As we made it to the entrance I saw Shar standing by the door and I took a deep breath and braced myself for a show-down but my sister had something else in mind.

"Oh hey Shar what are you doing all the way out here?" I looked at my sister like she was Courtney Love crazy; I then looked at Shar who had a big ass smile on her face something wasn't adding up. That bitch lied to me, she knew my sister all along. I guess my sister realized that I was lost so she introduced us.

"Hey Brynn this is Shar she's the receptionist at Felito's father recycling company, Shar this is my little sister Brynn the one I was telling you about."

"Umm and what exactly what were you telling this stranger Amelie?" I grilled Shar.

"Oh nothing Brynn, just that you were spoiled and that you couldn't find a man to save your life." she smirked.

Oh this bitch was slick but I'm much slicker. "Is that so? Amelie I would never guess that you'd be so cordial with the woman that's screwing your husband. I mean wow; he sure knows how to pick them." I handed my sister a manila envelope with the pictures I had Pam take of them hugging and kissing the other night and then I shot Shar a look that said "checkmate".

Amelie scanned the pictures and placed her hand over her mouth. I was waiting for her to send a fury of punches at Shar or even cuss her ass out but....

"Brynn how could you be so heartless?" was what came out her mouth next. She than commenced on cussing me out in front of Target all the while Shar looked on amused.

This was not what I planned and after I realized that my sister wasn't going to leave this fool I was more than ready to go. "You need to find yourself a hobby Brynn because this shit is for the birds." Amelie ranted. I swear that was the *hoodest* phrase my sister had ever uttered in her life.

I saw an old lady walking by with a smoothie in her hand and I quickly snatched that shit and threw it on Shar, the smirk that bitch was just sporting was now a thing of the past. I watched as she shrieked in horror along with a few onlookers including the old lady who was now without a smoothie. I handed her a ten-dollar bill and walked back to my car, and if Amelie was smart she'd be right behind my ass or she'd have to catch a cab. I learned a valuable lesson that day which was to mind my own goddamn business. Never again would I tell my sister anything concerning her man, and I meant that shit. He could be fucking another man and I wouldn't tell her dumb ass shit. The entire ride back to my mother's house was in silence which suited me just fine because I didn't have shit to say to her dumb ass.

Chapter 11

"Damn, are you serious? You did all that for nothing oh well fuck 'em." I nodded my head in agreement and continued to eat my shrimp Alfredo that Emilio had prepared for dinner. I learned in just the short time that we've been together that my baby was an excellent cook. He said his Abuela taught him how to cook but I didn't care who taught him because I was now reaping the benefits of it. I still didn't have a clue as to what he did for a living but by now I could really care less. He paid my mortgage, or so he thought. My house was three hundred thousand and I had a huge lawsuit last year that allowed me to pay it off in full. I only had utilities, car note and a few other miscellaneous bills. I couldn't have been happier. I loved this nigga no doubt about it.

Every once in a while, I would feel sorry for his dumb ass wife who had no clue, I mean I wondered how it made her feel when her husband didn't come home for a month straight? If I was her I would have been forced to divorce his ass and walk away with half. I stopped eating at her restaurant but Pam was still a regular at 'Onnie's Place' and I wasn't mad at her because the food was scrumptious. My thing was I'd be a damn fool for eating at her restaurant when I was sleeping with her husband. Emilio said that she didn't know about us but my intuition was telling me otherwise so I slept with my eyes half open. I had just finished cleaning up the dinner dishes when I heard the doorbell ring. Emilio had already stepped out for the night, he said he and Alex had to handle some business and he had a key so I knew it wasn't him. I dried my hands off went to open the door. As soon I opened it I was face to face with Onnie, Emilio's wife and she wasn't alone. How did this bitch know where I live?

"Brynn, honey how are you this evening may we come in?" Onnie asked in a polite tone and automatically I knew this wasn't about her husband. I looked over at the man she was with and realized that this was Nash, her brother but that still didn't explain what they were doing at my house.

"Umm sure come on in" I said as I led them into my sitting room. "Nash tells me that he sent you a message on Face Book and that you and him have been conversing so I figured why not drop by?" Onnie was as excited like a fiend with script of perc tens. I suddenly realized why Emilio cheated on her; the bitch is a control freak and overly aggressive. I never gave this bitch my phone number, let alone my address and she comes by unannounced with her brother. This bitch is a nut-case and would have to be handled with care.

"Oh and I got your address from Lilith your best friend. I think it's awesome that your best friend is your business partner. I use your hair care products; they are very good. I didn't even know that you were the CEO of the company until Pam pointed it out to me the other day while we were having lunch."

My brow raised is suspension. Since when did these two become lunch buddies? I was going to have to see what it was really hitting for. And as for Lilith she knew better than giving my shit out. "You have a lovely home what do you think Nash?"

Nash who had been sitting idly not saying a word finally spoke. "You have a very beautiful home Brynn. You have to excuse my sister she can be a bit overbearing at times. We were just in the area when the idea popped in her head to stop by; once again you have to excuse her." He stood up and shook my hand. "We'll be leaving now sorry for the interruption." Nash was not only sexy but he was very polite but that didn't excuse the fact that they were in my house uninvited. I walked them out and locked the door. What the fuck is going on? I picked up my iPhone to facetime Emilio but it didn't go though. I called and it went straight to voicemail. That nigga had a lot of explaining to do. The game had changed from checkers to chess and I was no one's pawn.

Chapter 12

I went over my parents' house the next day because my Aunt Ora was in town for the week and I wanted to chop it up with her for a bit. My Aunt Ora was my fucking idol; she was what every woman should be…free! She could dress her ass off too. She was my father's baby sister and also the most outgoing and I loved her for that. As soon as I walked in Amelie rolled her eyes at me and a pitiful looking Felito shook his head in disgust but I didn't give a fuck they could both fuck a goat for all I care. I had no idea why they spent so much at my parents when they had their own townhouse minutes away in Odessa.

"Brynn!" My aunt Ora exclaimed rocking the hell out an Eliza J floral cotton dress. It was so girlie with a hint of sex appeal the Kate Spade pumps set the outfit off. My aunt Ora looks rivaled a run way model, her milk chocolate complexion, almond shaped eyes and perfect bone structure gave her an exotic look. She reminded me of Cynthia from the Atlanta housewives. She wore her dark hair cut close in an abundance of short natural curls and she was forever twenty-one in her look when in actuality she was thirty-seven. My aunt definitely aged well.

"Auntie! How are you?"" I squealed as I hugged her tightly.

"Couldn't be any better honey and that's for sure feel me?" I looked at my aunt's nose piercing and smiled.

"Oh, hell yeah I feel you!"We burst out laughing and I heard my sister clear her throat.

"Ahem, lunch is ready come in the sunroom."

My aunt shot me a look that said a thousand words and we held hands as we walked inside the room. I sat across from Amelie and my aunt sat beside me. My father sat at the head of the table, as usual and my mother sat next to him. My stomach began to growl and I was more than ready to dig in on the rice and cream chicken that my mother prepared but Amelie had other things in mind.

"Brynn, I told mother what you had done to Felito and you should be lucky that he's not pressing charges against and your little hoodlum of a man, you've always been pathetic when it comes to men." My mother gasped and my father sat down his hanky and shot me a not-so happy glare. "You're the reason why he refused to have lunch with us today; he can't stand the sight of your pathetic ass!"

"Amelie that's enough!" my father yelled obviously not in the mood.

"Nah, it's okay daddy let her finish." I discreetly slipped off my pumps under the table. I already knew this bitch would try to break bad with me and I came prepared. This bitch was mad because her man was a lie and cheat and I was the one who brought it to her. Instead of thanking me, she hated me and I couldn't understand why. I picked up my fork and piled it with food took a huge bite and smiled, and my sister continued her ranting.

"You think you're so cute Brynn but you're not, you screw every Tom, Dick and Harry that comes your way and don't think twice about it. You're so uneducated and uncouth and I can't see how you're my real sister, I hate you!"

I was not impressed by Amelie's childish read. I would bet my bank account that this bitch was mentally delayed.

"Amelie that's seriously enough now can we enjoy our lunch?" My aunt Ora interjected as she nudged me under the table.

"Oh no this is your entire fault Ora! You taught her all that ghetto fabulous behavior!"

My aunt sat down her fork and got up to walk over to Amelie but I pulled her back down. My mother's face was flushed and my father's jaw started thumping but I didn't hear shit he was saying.

"Amelie, are you mad because your man is a cheater and he's sleeping with his secretary? Or is the fact that you could never fuck with me? You think I give a fuck that you hate me, bitch please. Aunt Ora isn't the reason why your man isn't satisfied; your dry ass pussy is. It's a wonder the skin on his dick ain't rub off from playing in your sand box. All those doctors you've been going to and your shit still can't get wet? I see why you hate me; look at me I'm a fucking BOSS literally. I have a man who's satisfied with all I give him; sorry I can't say the same about you."

Amelie smirked "Your man is *married* Brynn so that means your vagina isn't all that either at least somebody married me honey." The room suddenly became quiet so quiet that you could hear a mouse piss on cotton.

"Brynn is this true?" My mother finally asked after getting over the initial shock... "Is Emilio married?" All eyes were now all on me and instead of being embarrassed like most would be I smiled and held my head up high. I took a small sip of my wine and wiped the corners of my mouth with a handkerchief.

"Yes, it is mommy he is married...and what?" I leaned up against the curio cabinet with my arms folded in defiance. I knew they were about to play judge and jury but I had something for all their asses. I don't know how in the hell Amelie found out about his wife. It didn't even matter it was out there now. My father hit the roof and started yelling at me and my mother was rambling off in French. They had damned me to hell. My sister had a satisfied smirk on her face and my aunt Ora ate her food like a big bomb hadn't just been dropped. I sat up slowly and walked over to Amelie who still wore that smirk on her face and slapped the shit out of her. The slap was so loud that it sounded like dick fucking a wet pussy.

"That's for disrespecting my aunt bitch." Amelie who had no fight in her at all looked over at mother for support. I knew my mother was heated but I never expected her to haul off and smack me. She smacked me so hard that my face was numb. My daddy didn't do anything. I just put my shoes back on, grabbed my bag. I stood at the side of the table inches away from my mother who was now being held back by my father.

I started to laugh. "You know what I'm not even mad. Mommy you got your rocks off but you ain't slap Ms. Laurie when you caught Daddy fucking her in basement on the pool table. You ain't say shit when that DNA paper came in the mail for one of those chicks at the church that daddy be fucking." I turned to my father. "I love you so much. I would never disrespect you but you let this bitch put her hands on me...your favorite child as you claim. Did Mommy tell you that the reason why Chance doesn't come around because he enjoys fucking other men? Yeah, that nigga gets more dick in his mouth than a Hoe on New Castle Ave. He been getting dicked down since he was at Salesianum. Amelie is mentally retarded. She allows her sad ass husband to fuck ghetto bitches. Shit's not so sweet in the Davis household. We are not the fucking Huxtables. I don't care how much money, or how big of a house you live in you still have remnants of ghetto trash in you. So I suggest y'all cut the shit and keep it real. Stop running from who the fuck you are. I know who I am."

I turned on my heels and sashayed out the door. Fuck everybody. They wanted to tell secrets and treat me like I was a spawn I just spilled a large amount of raspberry tea all over their lily white carpet.

Chapter 13

On my way home I called Pam and cussed her ass out for telling Onnie where I lived and then I gave her the rundown of what just happened at my parent's house.

"So Amelie tried to break bad huh? Well at least you slapped the broad, when she broke bad with me everybody held my ass back because they knew I would have torn-dat-ass-up."

I couldn't help but to giggle.

"I still don't get why auntie slapped you though like what the fuck?"

"I don't even care Pam it's cool, but um I'll call you later." I didn't even wait for her reply before I hung up. I had just reached my house and I didn't want to do shit but sleep.

***

Emilio didn't come home that night and for once I didn't even care I was pissed off at my sister and mother and needed some time alone anyway. That night I ran some bath water and threw in some smelly bath salts and relaxed. I rolled me up a blunt of purple flowers and listened to my playlist on my phone. Old R&B played soothing my soul.

The following morning, I ran a few miles on the treadmill while watching the news. I just stepped off it when my doorbell rang. I hoped it wasn't my mother or my stupid ass sister because I'd hate to have to be rude but when I looked out the peephole I saw my aunt Ora standing outside the door and I quickly perked up and opened the door. We embraced before she took a seat and I smelled her favorite perfume, Chanel no. 5. She's been wearing that since I was a kid.

"I just came over to check on you Brynn yesterday was a crazy day are you alright?" Warm tears rolled down my check without permission and I quickly wiped them away.

"Aunt Ora, I don't know why or how but I love that man you know? For the first time in a long time I love somebody other than family and he has the nerve to be married I fucked up." I confessed.

She nodded her head in agreement and wiped my tears. "You don't have to tell me honey because believe me I've been there. I'm not ya momma so I'm not trying to lecture you but I did want to say be careful. I don't agree nor do I disagree with what you're doing but be careful. I'm not going to judge you because like Young said 'only god can judge me who the fuck are you? I'm guessing that whoever this man is he's treating you right and making you happy so I'm not going to tell you to leave him alone, but be careful dealing with a married man is borderline psychotic."

"What?"

"Yeah you heard me psychotic but instead of explaining my theory to you I'm going to let you find out on your own because your little ass is grown." She smirked, "But enough of that. Your sister almost got her mouth swollen talking crazy to me. That was foul for you to try and throw my brother under the bus like that. Nisa is not going to do nothing about Kevin. She already knew what time it was with him and Laurie. They were together since they were young. The reason why they weren't together being your daddy can't keep his dick in his pants. He found Nisa, who was a fucking mess might I add. She could barely speak proper English, her teeth where fucked up. She was trash, I mean trash for real. Kevin cleaned her up. He got those hideous teeth she had fixed along with a green card."

I interrupted her, "Green card?"

"Yes, honey your mother was illegal. Her entire family was. The reason why you don't see them is because they stay under the radar. Nisa has like two sisters that married American men. They're around here somewhere. If they see Nisa they wouldn't know who the hell she was. I'm telling you your mom was tore up. That's why I can't stand her ass. She forgot where she came from and Kevin will tell her quick she can go back. He made her ass sign a pre-nup. It's not like she could read to know what the hell was really going on. She tries to be prim and proper because she knows she really ain't shit but a trophy piece." She paused. "So her precious Chance is gay. I'm not surprised." She laughed.

My mind was still registering all she said about my mother. The information she delivered made me lose more respect for her. I couldn't stand people like that.

"Gay ain't the word. Chance is a Divo, honey. We talk twice a year. I have his car in my garage. Amelie and Mommy barely talk to him at all. I feel bad now because now since daddy knows the truth he's going to cut him off. You know how he is with religion. He almost killed me when he heard I was dabbling in that life."

"Girl, he chewed a new asshole into your mother and sister after you left. He was all up in Nisa face I had to stand in front of her to make sure he didn't whoop her ass. He sent Amelie home and told her not to come back until he said so. Then he had the nerve to send Nisa to her room. I was like what the fuck is going on in this bitch. He was handing out punishments like they were children. He was tight about Chance so tight that he took a drink. You know Kevin don't drink. He was hurt. He said Chance was no longer welcome in his home and he cut him off."

"I feel bad now. Poor Chance. Did my parents say anything about me I know my father was upset?"

She stared at me and smiled, "My brother loves you no matter what it's your mother whose acting retarded. Of course he isn't thrilled about your dealings with a married man and I can't lie neither am I but I don't have to live your life you do. He called asked me to stop by and talk to you about this guy you're seeing. He doesn't want anything happening to you."

Tears trickled down my face and this time with my permission. My Dad had every right to be mad at me as I never wanted to disappoint him but I loved him, Emilio is my man even if he is married. I knew that everybody wanted me to let him go including my aunt but I couldn't, he was a part of me, he was my sweetest sin, my beautiful nightmare and I refused to let him go. Just then my phone vibrated on the coffee table, it was a text from Emilio telling me he loved me. I couldn't help but to crack a smile, like that Roots song, he got me. I looked over at my aunt who was staring at me exquisitely and I knew that no matter what she had my back through thick and thin.

"I love you Aunt Ora and I'm going to ride this one until the wheels fall off."

"I love you too niece, and make sure you ride it right."

Chapter 14

It was officially the first day of summer and all the hot boys were out at the Getty with their bikes. I was on Market Street at the Getty Gas station getting a chicken and rice platter. Pam was enjoying the view and I was thinking about Emilio. Every little thing I did he was on my mind. Every night I would lie on his chest and listen to his heartbeat as we kicked it. We would talk for hours about any and everything and I never had that with anyone before. "These niggas are looking too good for me to be exclusive with one nigga, maybe I should explore my options and slow down with Alex for a week so I could catch me a youngin' what you think Brynn?" I looked over at my hoe-ass cousin and shook my head this bitch always thought with her pussy and never her head.

"Bitch you know that Alex will kill your ass I don't see how you even play around like that, that nigga is a fool."

Pam poked out her bottom lip. "I know Brynn but damn do you see this nigga though?" She pointed at a brown skinned man sitting on a Kawasaki bike and salivated over him. His face was shielded by a helmet but his body was ripped.

"How the hell can you tell when he's wearing a helmet Pam? You're just a hot ass!" I joked looking in the man's direction again.

"Call me what you want but don't call me blind bitch he is too fucking fine." She fanned herself and I laughed. A few seconds later a female rolled up on a similar bike, the only indication that it was a female was because of the long curly hair that sprinkled out from underneath the helmet. "Damn, Now I want a bike!" Pam whined after seeing the girl on the bike pop a wheelie. I had to admit from the back the girl had an ass that could swallow up a G-string. I mean I stopped lusting after women long ago but I had to admit, she was bad. Just as we were about to walk across to Rash's, the beauty supply store, the female pulled over by the curb and removed her helmet. I got the shock of my life when I saw that it was Onnie.

"Yo ain't that Onnie?" Pam yelled over the loud motorcycles.

"Hell yeah that's her." I said giving her the once over. "I don't remember her ass being that fat, Brynn I think she got ass shots." Pam said all the while I thought the same thing. The last time I saw her, her butt wasn't that chunky, I mean it was plump but now her ass is Black China fat. "Maybe it's because she can't keep her man home at night, Brynn." Onnie gave Pam an intense stare and placed her kickstand on and walked over to us. I looked over at Pam and she did a shrug I guess she was feeling like its whatever.

"I read lips very good Pam so what exactly are you implying about me and my husband? You must know something that I don't." After looking at her up-close for a few moments I also noticed that Onnie's teeth were veneers and perfect. They had to cost a grip damn this bitch was going all out huh? Pam sucked her teeth signaling her annoyance and I feared the worst. Pam's temper was worse than Naomi Campbell's. She once had a fight with a funeral usher about trying to seat her in the back when it was in fact her aunt that was lying in the casket.

"What the fuck you read lips now?" Pam shot, placing her cell phone in her clutch bag. Onnie closed her eyes, obviously trying to keep calm but I had a feeling that Pam was ready to get wreck.

"Damn Brynn, I see you're still beautiful as ever." It was Nash and I was grateful he intervened because I definitely didn't want shit to get out of hand.

"Oh how are you Nash?" I shot Pam a 'bitch chill' look and she quickly walked inside of the beauty supply store. I noticed as I conversed with Nash that Onnie was shooting me crazy daggers. It was almost like she could tell that I was screwing her husband but didn't want to say anything or maybe it was my conscience playing dirty tricks on me.

"So how about you let me take you out tonight? Anywhere you want to go?" I was shocked as hell I didn't expect Nash to be so bold and ask me out in front of his sister and from the looks she giving him I could see that she wasn't happy. So just to piss her off I agreed and placed my number in his phone.

"I'll see you later Nash, oh and nice bike Onnie I guess Nash will have to take me riding one day... later". I walked inside of the beauty supply store to find Pam. I knew she was pissed and I wanted to feel her out.

"That bitch got another thing coming if she thinks she gone come at me like that she's lucky I didn't lay her ass out in front of her brother. I'm not fucking her husband, but if she wants a problem I'll give her one." I couldn't help but to laugh. Pam is a fucking nut case. She grabbed a pack of bobby pins and placed it on the counter. "I'm dead ass serious, Brynn." I shook my head in agreement. No words were needed because I knew she was serious.

"Where did you say you're going tonight?" Emilio asked me as I dressed. I was adding the final touches to my make-up looking at my reflection in the mirror. Emilio hadn't been spending quality time with me lately and I wasn't feeling that shit so I decided to go out with Nash like I agreed earlier. To get some payback, I was going out with Nash despite the fact that I knew Emilio wouldn't like it.

"Mommy, you got this short ass dress and smelling like good pussy where the fuck do you think you're going?" he ran his hand up my dress and tickled my clit.

"Stop it bae I'm going out because you've been neglecting me lately and was sup with your wife she was real saucy with her mouth today?" I just had to ask. "You still fucking her?" I was becoming angry just by the thought of him still touching her when I was all he needed.

"What?" he huffed all the while still rubbing on my clit making me buckle. He stood up and pushed me down on the bed with a roughness that turned me the fuck on. He ran his tongue across my neck and I felt my pussy dampen and his warm breath tickled my skin and I was ready to submit to him but first.

"Eat my pussy." I demanded as he pulled my dress down. He flashed me his million-dollar smile and dove in face first into my sweetness. One thing I couldn't deny is that he's a pussy monster. He slurped up my juices and rubbed his face all in my honey as I fucked his face. I wanted to suffocate the nigga for pleasuring me so well but since I wanted some dick I'd let him live. He got up and wiped his face and flipped me over on my back and penetrated me with so much force that I gasped in shock but there wasn't near dick I couldn't take. I was coming when he quickly pulled out of me and demanded I suck it. He had his hands on his hips with his long thickness swinging like he was King Kong or somebody. I sat up on the bed and crawled towards the edge of the bed and I gripped him with my right hand and cuffed his balls with my left. I took all of him into my mouth and looked up at him hoping that he had his eyes on me but he was too busy enjoying himself to be looking down at me but that didn't stop my show. I just slurped up his dick like some soup and then I placed is balls in my mouth. That's when his knees began to buckle and I knew I had him where I wanted him. You see I still planned on going out with Nash and I knew that the easiest way of getting Emilio out my hair was to give him a good shot and some bomb ass head.

"Damn baby." he moaned and I took him out my mouth and opened my legs up wide, inviting him in. He licked his lips, and smiled. That nigga was whipped so I whipped it on him real good and after I finished I washed my kitty and left his ass sleeping on my bed.

My date with Nash was cooler than I expected and I couldn't help but to notice how paid he was. When he paid the bill he paid with a Platinum Ritz-Carlton metal American Express Card. Either the Air force paid him well or he was hustling, either way I didn't care I just wanted some information out of him. I wanted to know all about Onnie with her funny acting ass. We were headed back to my car which was parked in front of his house in New Castle when he started telling me his life story, which I really didn't want to hear but if it included Onnie then I was all ears.

"Onnie and I grew up in Newark, New Jersey in the Iron bound section it was bad but not bad as it is today. We were raised by my mother and Abuela. He looked over at me and I nodded for him to continue. "My father was always in and out of jail and he and Onnie never got along. At first I couldn't understand why but I found out later on…" He looked straight ahead and I immediately knew that this was a touchy situation but I wanted to know more. He cleared his throat and continued. "He was raping her every morning before we went to school. He waited until my mother left for work to do it of course, and since we didn't share rooms I wasn't aware of what was going on until one day I walked in her room to wake her up for school and her sheets were bloody and she was crying hysterically." I rubbed his hand and told him that he didn't have to continue the story if he didn't feel up to it but he told me it was alright. "I was fifteen and Onnie was only twelve, I tried to kill his ass! But my mother stopped me. Don't you know she actually took his side and said that Onnie was too grown for her own good? My mother's family is from Cuba and they never really liked my Mexican father so I made one phone call to my uncle Fernando over in Cuba and within 24 hours my father was taken care of. My mother was very upset with me after that so she kicked me out but deep down inside she was grateful, my father did her more harm than good anyway. I moved in with my grandmother and I had Onnie come with me. My mother eventually remarried but by this time she wanted nothing to do with us. She was still grieving over my father but by that time I didn't give a fuck. After I graduated from high school I went into the service and Onnie was in love with Emil." My ears perked up at the mention of my baby.

"You mean Emilio?" I just had to ask.

He looked over at me and smiled. "Back then we called him Emil and shit I still do but now he prefers Emilio. Emil was a good dude so I didn't mind him dating my little sister especially since he's older than I am." He chuckled and I had to laugh too because I never did ask Emilio how old he was.

"Nash how old are you if you don't me asking?" we had just pulled up in front of his house and I wasn't anywhere finished talking to him but I knew that I'd have another chance at it. "I'm thirty-three is that too old for you Brynn?" That meant Emilio was at least thirty-five damn.

"Um no that's fine, the older the man the more experienced right?" I shot him a crooked grin.

"If you say so." Was his only reply and I was thinking maybe I said something that he didn't agree with.

"Don't take this the wrong way. I thought y'all were niggas...I mean African American. Onnie doesn't look-never mind." I was starting to sound stereotypical. I thanked him for the date and went to open the door when he grabbed my arm.

"Look Brynn, I'm sorry about that I was just thinking about my ex-wife she used to say that too and when you said it, I got flashbacks." He looked so adorable and I felt my pussy throbbing which was totally unexpected. Like I said before Nash is a looker. He has long curly eyelashes and his mocha skin is blemish free. Hands down this nigga is fine. "It's okay Nash but I had fun tonight I got to get going it's getting late." He looked like he wasn't ready for me to leave but if I wanted to keep my pussy intact I had to leave. Nash is definitely something I'd try under different circumstances.

"But you didn't tell me your life story..." he whined and I laughed.

"Maybe next time, Nash." He walked me to my car and kissed my cheeks. "Hopefully next time is sooner than later, goodnight." I drove off with thoughts of Nash on my mind and that was unusual since I usually only thought of Emilio.

Chapter 15

I filled Pam in on the date I had with Nash the night before and she was shocked. "I can't believe you really went out with him what did you tell Emilio?"

I sucked my teeth, "Emilio is not my husband and I didn't tell his ass anything, shit." I grumbled I couldn't believe this bitch had the audacity to say some shit like that to me. My other line beeped. It was my mother's cell number. I told Pam I'd call her back.

"Can I help you?"

"Brynn, you're my daughter and we need to make this right. Our family is falling apart. I can't continue to live this way. It's killing me." My mother pleaded."

I rolled my eyes and huffed.

"You are shortening your days by disrespecting me. It's in the bible." She said.

I laughed to myself. This woman was a nutcase.

"This is all Ora's fault she fed you poison about me since you were a child. Her and that-that whore Laurie. They ruined this family."

I instantly caught an attitude, "How so?" I snapped. "How so? Ora nor Laurie didn't have anything to do with it." I defended my favorite aunts.

"Hell if she didn't, she made you believe it was okay to sleep with married men and she's been corrupting your brain since you were a child. You *and* Pam. Poor child has been a slut since she was nine. Laurie was sleeping with my husband in my home. It's a wonder Lilith didn't turn into a whore as well!" I was appalled, I knew my mother didn't care much for Pam but she was taking it a little too far only I could talk bad about her.

"Ma, now your tripping that is not true! Pam has nothing to do with you, neither does Lilith. From what I heard you have no room to talk. You were nothing but a dirty illiterate immigrant until daddy came." She hung up in my ear. Before I could get my thoughts together Emilio grabbed me from behind.

"I see you like playing games Brynn." I frowned up my face.

"Nah, don't do that. When you frown you're not pretty mommy. I know about your date with Nash."

Instead of denying it I stood in silence his arms were still wrapped around my waist and I could smell the minty toothpaste on his breath.

"Onnie told me, what's really good with you tho? You trying to get that nigga killed?" he said pulling his gun from his waist and sitting it on the dresser.

My eyes widened at the sight of the chrome steel. "He's your brother in law baby why would you say something like that?" I finally asked, removing his hands from around my waist.

"You think I give a fuck?"

I shook my head no and he continued.

"Everybody has to die sometime right? Just don't get that nigga killed sweetheart." He kissed me passionately and told me he had to work. I still didn't know what this nigga did for a living shit. I guess Nash would have to tell me. I sent him a text message telling him to meet me at Brandywine Park at the fountain near the zoo. That was a secluded area. I knew that seeing him was risky business but I was needed to know some things and I knew Nash would be the one to tell me. I threw on a pair of jean shorts and a PINK crop top and a pair of pink and white air max I got from the Villa the other day. I had a 2011 Mustang 5.0 that belonged to my brother Chance. I decided to drive that since no one ever seen it like that. I was on some creep shit. I did a lot of things but having someone's murder on my conscience was not going to be one of them.

Nash was a damn good rock skipper. I know it sounds whack but we needed to do something to move time.

"So you want to know my business huh?" I asked Nash as we decided to grab a seat at a picnic table and relax.

He laughed, "I wouldn't call it that but yeah tell me something about yourself, and I already know that you have your own business so tell me something that I don't know." Nash was looking sexy in a black tee and jean shorts. The new Jordan's sneakers were blazing and I couldn't help but to study them and made a mental note to order a pair for myself and Emilio.

"My mother is from Sierra Leone and my father is from Wilmington. I have an older brother and sister and I love Caribbean food." I looked at him and waited for him to say something but he remained quiet so I guess he was waiting on me to continue. "Um what else you want to know Nash?"

He looked deeply in my eyes and smiled. "Everything Brynn." He reiterated in an even tone. This nigga was staring to get too deep for me I didn't want to establish a real friendship with him but he was making it hard for me not to. He realized that I wasn't ready to share anything else with him. He went to his car and pulled out a picnic basket. I blushed when I saw it. He came back pulled out a dark blue plastic table cloth and began to set the table. I thought he had hand made the sandwiches until I opened them up. They were packed with meat. This nigga went to Olympics to get the subs. I liked Olympics but to me Brown Bag was better. We started talking about life in the military. I was glad for that and then he started getting serious again.

"You know why I confessed to you my past last night?" He asked while I snacked on a krimpet tasty cake.

"Why?"

"Because I feel like I can be myself with you. I feel like you're someone I can share my life with." I nearly choked on the cake that I was eating.

"Excuse me?"

"Don't get bent out of shape Brynn I didn't mean like that by no means am I ready for anything besides friendship."

"Oh." I was relieved. He laughed loudly and I didn't find a damn thing funny. "What's so funny?" He stopped laughing, looked at me and laughed again. I was getting agitated and I wanted to know what the fuck was so funny.

"It's nothing, it's just that my sister said you were full of yourself and she was right but it's cute I'm not mad at you."

I was livid. "Your sister? How the hell would she know that if she barely knows me?" I snapped. This nigga and his sister got me fucked up, if anything I'm full of her husband's semen but nothing else.

Nash could tell that I was slightly offended and he softened up. "My sister is jealous of you Brynn, maybe that's why she said it. I don't know why and I don't really care you're cool with me and that's all that matters okay?" I calmed down.

"Okay but you better chill because I got a chopper in the car!" We both laughed at my statement and I acted like nothing happened. I couldn't even be mad at him because I heard that all my life, plus he said Onnie was jealous of me that alone had me walking on the moon. So I did get under her skin- I loved it. About an hour later I ended our little outing and drove to my parents' house to have a long talk with my mother. I was feeling good so I decided to go make amends with her stupid ass. The news that Onnie was jealous of me was the highlight of my day.

Chapter 16

I turned into my parents' development and there were state police cars, EMT's and a few undercovers everywhere. That was odd because nothing ever happened down here. I rode passed the townhouses where my sister lived and glanced up her street. I noticed my dad's Cadillac was there along with an undercover cop car. I hit the brakes and backed up then turned up her street. My heart was racing I prayed everything was ok with the kids. Baby Ciara was born with a severe case of asthma. The heat has been serious the last few days I hoped she is good.

I pulled up behind my father's car and hopped out the car and ran to the house. I was stopped by a white guy dressed in a tacky blue suit. I knew his ass was hot its a hundred degrees out and this nigga got on a three piece.

"Ma'am, stop right here this is a crime scene." He stated.

"I don't give a fuck what it is. This is my sister's house and I'm about to go see what the hell is going on." Anxiety and anger didn't mix well with me. If he didn't let me through I was about to catch a serious charge. He reached out like he was about to put his hands on me and my father walked out the house. The look on his face was like he had seen Lucifer himself. His eyes were swollen. He looked weak.

"Daddy! Daddy!" I yelled. He looked up.

"Brynn," He held is arms out. I ran past the detective and embraced him.

"What's wrong? What happened? Are the babies ok?" I held on him for dear life. Something was wrong and it was bad- real bad. I could feel it.

He walked me inside of my sister's house. The house was a wreck blood was splattered everywhere. The mirrors were broke. The crime lab was inside combing through evidence. I felt like I was about to throw up. My beautiful day had turned into a bloody nightmare. I looked at my father and stared him in the eyes he broke down in tears.

"Oh God daddy. What happened? She's not gone is she? Then it hit me where was my mother. She was nowhere in sight.

"Where's mommy?" I shouted. He wrapped his arms around me.

"She's fine. She-she found them."

"Found who?" I cried.

"Amelie and Felito. They were both beaten badly. Melie will make it but she looks so bad. My baby…" He broke down in the living room and clutched his heart.

"Oh my God! Somebody help! Help me." I screamed. The EMT's rushed to his side pushing me away.

The detective I met outside came to me and rested his hand on my shoulder. "Ma'am, I know this is a bad time but I need to ask you a few questions about your sister and deceased brother-in-law."

I faced him.

"Deceased? Felito's dead." I whispered.

His face was flushed. "I'm sorry ma'am; I thought your father told you. Mr. Rodriquez was shot in the head execution style after he and your sister was beaten and left for dead. The children are unharmed they are at A.I. DuPont being checked over now. I need you to come down to the station."

"I can't leave my father!" I couldn't believe this was happening. My dad was having some type of attack, Felito was dead and Amelie….God. I knelt down on the ground in prayer position.

"Detective Levy, you need to see this!" An officer wearing plastic gloves came out with an envelope that looked like an invitation of some sort. The detective pulled out a pair of gloves and carefully opened the letter.

"What the fuck…" he said.

He opened the envelope and pulled out a letter. The words: When she stops I will stop...was typed on it. The detective read it again. "I think we have a problem on our hands...."

Chapter 17

Onnie

On the outside looking in I would seem to have the picture perfect life. As they say, *all things are not as they seem*. The last drip of water dispersed into the ceramic pink coffee mug from my favorite and most used appliance; my Keurig. I drank coffee as often as a fiend shot dope. I couldn't get enough of it. Besides the occasional Xanax, a strong brew of Colombian Coffee made my day go smoothly. The situations I had to endure permitted me to indulge in something more potent; I chose the latter.

I opened the lid carefully removed the piping hot K-cup and tossed it in the trash. The bright sun crept through the closed drapery. I pulled them together not allowing any light to seep through. I retrieved my cup took a sip of the hot liquid which stirred through my body rapidly like lava. A sense of tranquility overcame me. Satisfied, I took a seat on the plush chocolate antique chaise which was located in the library-my sanctuary. I closed my eyes and allowed my body to get lost in the plush pillows. It's a shame but lately this is the only way I sensed comfort. My *husband* had become detached sort of a nostalgia.

His behavior is not something new. I had become accustomed to it. No one is aware of the anguish I have to withstand. If they did they wouldn't believe it. Emilio is an outstanding citizen who gives hope to those who are in despair. His donations to the Alfred I. Children's hospital earned him a golden plaque embedded on their wall of sponsors. The Back to school and Christmas drives that he holds annually opens doors for him to participate in many lucrative adventures. I am the trophy wife standing by his side looking like I had just stepped off a runway in Milan. Smiling, kissing unfortunate children, visiting babies, mentoring battered women; it's all in vain. A façade. The smiles are phony and my words are empty. I sold my soul to Diablo at the tender age of sixteen. I am living a dark fairy tale that will not have a happy ending. There is no prince charming to rescue me.

"Onnie," Nash's deep voice echoed through the corridors. I took a few more sips of coffee before answering him.

"I'm in the library." I placed the mug on a coaster to avoid staining the imported hand carved table that Emilio purchased during our trip to Belize. Nash opened the door with a bottle of half-drunken water in hand. The white *wife beater* styled tank top was

106

saturated with sweat as well as the loose fitting black basketball shorts.

"Let me guess you either took advantage of the magnificent walking trail or you played a lonely game of b-ball on the full court out back."

He pulled the step ladder away from the eight foot high bookshelf and took a seat. "I ran suicides and did my morning exercise's on the court. That's my morning routine. I've been doing it for over ten years; I don't think that will ever change." He took another gulp of the water.

"A military man at heart. How did your little date go with Brynn yesterday? You came in rather late I take it that it went well." I sat up and waited for him to spill the gossip. He didn't get in until after midnight. Hopefully he was able to get to know her *very* well. "So, what's the juice? Did you hit?"

He smiled. He took the towel that was on his shoulder and began to wipe the beads of sweat from his forehead. "I don't kiss and tell Onnie, you know that." He grinned. "But no I didn't *hit*. We had a picnic and talked."

I frowned my face, "Talk...you didn't get in until after midnight and all you did was talk?" I didn't buy that story at all. My brother was fine. The vibe I got from Brynn didn't depict her as the look and not touch type.

"I just met her Onnie! I don't stick my dick in every available pussy out there. I have morals. I believe in doing things correctly. You should know that by now." His face hardened. "Why are you so worried about it anyway? Does this have anything to do with Emil?"

"Excuse me? Why would Emilio have anything to do with her? He barely knows the girl. I happen to think she would be good for you. She's smart and she is the CEO of her own company. She seems a bit lonely and I would like to be friends with her, however you know I don't believe in mingling with single people unless it's for business. I want us to be able to have double dates. Plus she's super cute...don't you think?"

He blushed. "She is beautiful. I like spending time with her I do want to get to know her better. I want to do it on my own terms not you dictating my every move." He got off of the ladder. "You should focus on giving me a niece or nephew and keeping that man of yours home more often. I've been here for almost a month and every time I come over here he's never here. What's up with that?"

I rolled my eyes, "Emilio is a busy man. We don't have time for children at this time. I opened my restaurant. I'm thinking about expanding. I just don't have time. You smell go home or go upstairs and get in the shower." I quickly changed the subject. I picked up the coffee cup and it slipped from my hand crashing to the ceramic floor.

"Are you ok? You're shaking." He placed his hands around mine.

I snatched away, "I'm fine. I have to get this mess up before it stains my floors. The cleaning service won't be here until Monday." I started to remove the broken pieces from the floor.

He grabbed hold of my arms, "Sis, calm down. Let me get the broom and clean this up for you. You're shaking, I'm afraid you may cut yourself. Is everything ok?" He took the broken pieces from my hands and placed them on the table. "Do you want to talk about it?" He caressed my back and squeezed my shoulder.

"I need-I..."Before I could finish my phone rang. Emilio's picture popped on the screen.

"*Yes,*"

"*Turn on the news.*" The phone went dead.

"Nash, hand me the remote off the shelf."

He handed it to me, "What's going on?"

I turned the television on the local news station. *Breaking News...yesterday afternoon in Middletown, Delaware the body of Felito Rodriquez and his brutally beaten wife Amelie Rodriquez was found in their home. The couple's children were reported missing and have been found in front of the new popular Caribbean Café restaurant located in the Christiana Mall. The children appeared unharmed but have been taken to A.I. DuPont Children's hospital to be examined. Full coverage of this story will be aired at noon.*

"Onnie, that's your restaurant they're showing! Wait a minute...Brynn has a sister named Amelie.

Oh God I need to call her." Nash ran out the room. I sat there gazing blankly at the television. I said a silent prayer for the family and for myself. Something wasn't right. "He's changed the game..." I said softly. Now I had to make sure he didn't win.

Chapter 18

Controlled chaos is how I would describe the scene before me. My dear father's face had turned from rich chocolate to ash. He looked worse than the people they showed on the *Save the Children* commercial. Poor Nisa was in the hospital room sitting in a wheelchair with an oxygen mask on portraying to be two seconds away from meeting her maker. Amelie laid in the bed in restraints heavily sedated. The beating she suffered was bad but at least she didn't end up like Felito. He was in the basement on a slab with a toe tag. I knew I was coming across a bit taciturn. Once the Detective revealed the mysterious letter, I knew this was some shit Felito caused.

Only those mafia people used that *Kiss of Death* shit. Everyone knew that Felito's family was knee deep in with those Italians. Now my sister was a widow laying in the bed looking like Rocky Dennis. What made my ass itch is how they left my precious niece and nephew in the mall for the taking. Thank God Shock was coming out of Onnie's restaurant and recognized them. He called me and I immediately let the detective know. Now they have him down at troop two questioning him like a fucking criminal and he was the one who saved them. The fake ass Dick Tracy motherfucker had the nerve to question me like I had something to do with it. I cussed his cracker ass out. Why would I have my sister beat up, even though I wanted to trash her on several occasions; I would never put innocent children in danger.

"Brynn, can you go to the children's hospital and get the babies. I need you to promise me to take care of them in case *we* don't make it." My mother removed the mask long enough to explicate her *dying* request. She gasped between each word as if it were draining the little life she imagined she had left out of her. I massaged the sides of my head as I struggled to conjoin the correct words to say without causing her mental to be in a more delusional state than it already was.

I took a deep breath as I moved closer to Amelie's bedside. I chose to stand by the door because her face was unbearable to look at. God knows when she came through she is going to need a shot of Thorazine to help her cope. Nisa was slumped in the chair heaving and wheezing. I swear this was a scene from a soap opera.

"For starters you nor Amelie is going to die. She's just a little banged up and her ego will be fucked up until the wounds heal. Give it a month or two and she will be good as new. As for you mother dear a Xanax will fix you right up. There is nothing wrong with you. Well let me rephrase that you are not going to die. I cannot promise you I will take care of the babies. Felito's family is at the hospital right now and I'm sure they will keep them until you snap back to reality. I suggest you do that soon because I bet any amount of money they are the reason why their son is dead."

She dropped the mask to her lap. "You are a horrid child! Do you have no sense of family? We are in the middle of a tragedy and you can't take the time out to help? How dare you speak about Felito's family in that manner! They wouldn't do anything to hurt Amelie or the babies. Why would they harm their own son? Nothing you are saying is logical. How don't we know *you* didn't have anything to do with it? Amelie told me you had that thug boyfriend of yours attack Felito. It's mighty funny that they find the babies at his *wife's* restaurant. Did you let the Detective know that bit of information?" She glared at me and I sneered at her. If we weren't in that hospital with a million State boys I would have grabbed her up out of that chair by the throat. "Oh just as I thought. You're protecting him and probably yourself as well."

I rushed over to her with my fist bawled up. My father snapped out of his trance in the nick of time. He hurried and stood in front of Nisa to protect her.

"You know what lady-you are pathetic. You sit up here and put on a show. It's not about you, honey. Yes, your dirty dick son in-law is dead. He had it coming to him. You and Amelie turned blind eye to the fact that he was cheating on her and his entire family is running drugs. It was inevitable that some shit was going to hit their doorstep. You need to thank God that she's alive. It could have been worse. So don't throw that guilt you're carrying on me and my *man*. That's their shit. I love the babies to death but I didn't lie down and birth them motherfuckers so it's not my responsibility to take care of them."
Both of my parents looked at me as if I were a stranger. They had no words. I was cool with that because they were going to fall upon death ears anyway. I turned away and headed out the door. They fucked up my mental and I needed a fix. On the way to the elevator I dialed Emilio…my vice.

***

"Ummm…right there daddy," I was lying flat on my stomach clawing the emerald green Egyptian thread sheets while Emilio appeased my appetite. Each stroke dissipated every ounce of misery that embedded itself in my being.
When I called him from the hospital he was already in our bed awaiting my arrival. The aroma of sweet orange from the Canova Aromatherapy candles

consumed the bedroom. I didn't have to say a word he stripped me naked and had his way with me. I had ventured into another world, a world free from my overbearing dysfunctional family. It was only me and Emilio surrounded by orange blossoms, blue skies and white fluffy clouds.

"I love you," He whispered in my ear. "You're mine. Do you understand me?"
I didn't answer him right away. I was too busy enjoying the slaying he was putting on my pussy.

"Brynn, I swear to you. I will kill anyone who tries to take you away from me. Anyone." His voice was rough and he sped up his pace and drove deeper inside me. Pain shot through my pelvic area instead of telling him to stop I pleaded for more. He grabbed the back of my neck pressing my head to the bed and shot his load inside of me. My body shook violently from the euphoria I experienced. He rolled off of me to his side of the bed and pulled me close to him. I kept my eyes closed trying to recapture the moment. There was a buzzing sound coming from the top of my night stand. It was my phone. I reached over and turned it off without looking to see who was calling. It didn't matter the only person I wanted to hear from was lying next to me right where he belonged.

Chapter 19

I woke up expecting to go another round with my love. To my surprise I was alone. I slid out of my bed and almost buckled to the floor when I attempted to stand. I giggled and went to the bathroom. I sat on the toilet to pee and my coochie was throbbing. I looked down between my legs and it looked as if someone punched my pussy lips in the face. They were swollen and red. I took the tissue and dapped lightly. "Damn he beat the pussy up…up…up." I sang. I flushed the toilet went over to the tub setting the temperature to hot. I went to the cabinet and grabbed the box of Epsom salt. My whole body was in pain. I poured the contents into the water and then went to retrieve my cell phone from the table. I placed my hair in a bun on top of my head before stepping into the hot water.

I stuck my big toe in first to make sure I didn't injure myself. That's all I would need is nasty blisters making me look like a herpes victim. I tested the waters it was all good so I let my body slide down inside the tub. My skin tingled from the heat causing me to want to scratch an itch that didn't exist. Once I was comfortable I turned on my Galaxy Note and scrolled down the missed calls. Majority of them were from Nash and Pam, two from Shock and one from a blocked caller. I contemplated who I was going to call first. I knew if I chose Pam that bitch was going to talk until my bathwater turned cold. Nash was going to play twenty questions. I'm sure they all saw what happened since it was spread across the news.

To my surprise there wasn't a single call from Lilith, my business partner, my day one-sister-my best friend. I dialed her number to see what was up with her. She should have been the first person to ring my phone.

"Yes…" she answered displaying a lack of eagerness to talk.

"Why haven't I heard from you? Didn't you hear what happened? My sister was attacked the kids kidnapped and Felito is dead!"

Silence.

"Hello!"

No response.

I removed the phone from my ear to make sure my cheek didn't accidently hang up on her. That was one thing I hated about touch screen phones. You could have a whole conversation with air because you ended a call and ain't even know it. She was still on.

"Lilith, I know damn well you hear me! Hello!"

"Oh my God, give me a minute I had you on mute Hov was trying to tell me something." She seemed to be bothered and I had no idea why. I was the one who should be upset with her ignorant ass. I didn't give a fuck about no damn Hov or what he had to say. *"I went up to the hospital to check on Amelie yesterday. Your mother asked me to get the kids since you refused to do it. I tell you Brynn you can be really selfish. Your sister just lost her husband and your mother is sick. You could really help out it's not like you're at work or anything."*

No this Bitch didn't. I know she didn't say I didn't work. I'm the one who put the company together if it weren't for me her and that sorry ass husband of hers wouldn't have shit. I had to take a few breathes before I responded because her feelings were about to be hurt in a major way.

"Look, I'm not going to go there with you. I don't know what the fuck is eating you up but no one told your ass to take those kids the fuck home. You are the one who wanted to play fucking Saint Mary. I'm gonna let that slick ass comment go about me not working. How does that saying go, don't bite the hand that feeds you or you'll find yourself in a fucking soup kitchen..."

"That's not how it goes..." she interjected.

"That's how it goes with me!" I wanted to punch her smart ass through the phone. I knew she was showing off for that grape ape ass lookin' nigga.

"Brynn, I'm not going to be in for the rest of the week since I have to take care of your sister's children. You're going to have to go in yourself or get someone else to take care of your duties. Mine are already covered."

"They go to daycare. You don't need to sit home with them. If it's a safety issue they can go with your mom. Don't use my niece and nephew as a way out of work. You got vacation time. Take it. I'll make sure I'll document all that. What you need two weeks, a month...FMLA? Let me know because I can make it happen with a click of a button." I had to let her know she wasn't making no noise. I was the boss at the end of the day what I said went. I loved her to death but she didn't stop my flow. There were too many young ambitious girls without the baggage she carried who would love to be in her position.

"You know what do what you like. I don't have too..." There was a ruffling sound then I hear his raspy voice sounding like he smoked a carton of old ass *Pall Malls. "Man fuck you and that pussy ass job. You not gonna keep on son'n my wife. I take care of my family. You wouldn't have shit if it wasn't for her. We got lawyers on deck you don't want to see me. I ain't Lilith I don't have no soft spot for your whore ass!"*

I couldn't do nothing but laugh. This nigga was a fucking joke. He didn't even have a job. He was still trying to live out his street dreams and was damn near thirty. He was still a corner boy.

"Yo, Ravon watch your mouth son. You're talking real heavy. You can't even afford an attorney. What you using the money that I pay your wife with to sue me. Fuck out of here. You lucky I love Lilith and my god son, because your ass can take a permanent vacation...feel me? Don't ever fix your big lips to talk reckless to me again. I'm a let you live in your glory and allow your wife to think you got with me. You enjoy your day nigga...and oh yeah people don't blow Reggie no more step your game up." I hung up the phone. Something was in the motherfucking air because niggas was really high and if they didn't get it together quick I was going to have to bring them down to reality real quick.

Chapter 20

I hadn't heard from Emilio all day. I called his phone several times. I guess he had to go home to his wife. That shit made me ill every time I thought about it. I was in love with that nigga. I sat in my room all day thinking about the shit he said when he was blowing my back out. I chalked it up as some sadistic pillow talk shit. That was probably some shit he would say to random dumb broads to keep them in check. Pam called earlier in the day telling me about everything that happened at the hospital when I left. My ear had become numb I told her to come over because I wasn't in the mood for a six hour phone session. Nash called too. I sent him a text message telling him I was good I just needed a little space.

Truth was I thought it was nice that he showed mad interest in me. I decided to see him again I needed a few days to rest first. I can't lie, the conversation I had with Lilith and Gorilla Hov busted me. She and I never beefed heavy like that. I was going to let things die down and go talk to her. I wasn't going to apologize because I didn't do shit wrong. She was out of pocket. Everyone knew I didn't do kids like that. With Emilio in my life kids were not an option. I was too busy swinging from that big brown dick.

The door-bell rang I got up off the couch and carefully went to the door. The bath helped some but I still couldn't put my legs together when I walked. I opened the door and Pam was on her phone yelling at her mother. I hated when she did that. Ora was my favorite aunt. I wished she was my mother. Pam had no respect for her at all.

"Ok, shit!" she yelled before pushing the end button.

"Keep talking crazy to my aunt and I'm going to bust your teeth out."

She sucked her teeth. "Whatever. How you know I was talking to her anyway?" She strutted through the door wearing a pair of silver six inch t-strapped heels. They looked awfully familiar. I laughed to myself. She attempted get shoes like the ones I wore to her house when I met Alex and Emilio.

"You tried it," I laughed.

She plopped down on the end of the couch. "What?" she said twirling strands of the natural styled weave. The hair was so thick it reminded me of Chaka Khan in that I'm every woman video. All she needed was a flower on the side of her head and she would have had the look. The lime green romper wasn't helping. I eased slowly down on the other side of the couch and propped my feet on the ottoman. My shit was still sore there was no getting around it. I didn't even put on any panties because I didn't want anything rubbing against it.

Pam had her lips twisted as she studied my movement.

"Why you lookin' at me like that?" I cocked my head sarcastically.

"I'm trying to figure out what type time you on? I know that Amelie be on some shit and you can't stand the fuck nigga Felito but the kids though?" She rolled her eyes shaking her head.

I knew damn well she wasn't trying to judge no one. I saw her do more to her own mother. She forged checks, identity fraud and some more shit, not because she needed it but because some no good ass nigga she was stuck on when she was nineteen put her up to it. I hated her for a good year when she did that. Ora should have called the cops instead she whooped her ass like she was a stranger in the street. It took five serious ass whooping's and a broken jaw before she stopped. I believe if she tried her mother one more time we would have been pulling out our black dresses.

"If you came here to try and make me feel some type of way for not getting them you can go back out that door. I'm not for that shit today. I don't understand why people want to make me out to be the bad guy. I love my sister and yes I am upset about what happened. I was fucked up when I first pulled up over it. Then the detective found this letter with a stamp of a black kiss on it. It had a note saying, *I'll stop when she stops*. I knew it was some shit with Felito. You know his family is shiesty as fuck. It may have something to do with the Shar bitch. We did just confront her ass. Then the babies being taking and *unharmed*? That was some other shit. They got who they wanted because they would have killed Amelie too. Her face is just fucked up and that will heal in time."

"I don't know Brynn, some shit ain't right. I went up to the hospital and Aunt Nisa is swearing that Emilio has something to do with it. She told Uncle Kevin that she was going to tell the detective what happened with him and Felito. She's really upset about everything. They are waiting for Amelie to wake up so they can ask her if she remembers anything. You know she is going to be fucked up about Felito. She worshipped that nigga. I do know this though…it wasn't Emilio because he was with Alex all day. They went to Jersey and they went back again this morning. Alex told me they would be there for a few days. They have deliveries coming."

Now that was news to me. Emilio didn't say anything about going out of town and being gone for a few days. This was the type of stuff that had my head fucked up about him. Why did Alex feel free to tell Pam shit and Emilio told me nothing about his business? Maybe he really wasn't feeling me as much as I thought he was. My stomach started to knot up. I slumped down in the sofa and turned my head away from Pam. I was about to cry and I didn't want her to see me break down over some nigga I really had no ties too.

Pam placed her hand on my leg. "You alright cuzz?"

I nodded my head because if I opened my mouth the tears and emotions were going to flow.

"I think you should call Shock and at least say thank you. I saw him out at the hospital when I was leaving. He was looking good as shit too. He must have been in the gym because his chest was bulging through that Polo shirt and his arms were on point. Girl I thought thumper was in my pussy the way it was pounding. I don't know why you let his ass go. He look like he can fuck. Shit if you know like I know you would keep that nigga in your side pocket right next to the pussy. Cause at the end of the day Emilio is married to that stupid bitch Onnie and who knows what the fuck he be doing when he out of town-Alex included." She picked up the remote and turned on the television.

I whipped my head in her direction sat up in my seat, "What the fuck is that supposed mean? Emilio fucking somebody else?" I was livid. I know damn well he better not have been cheating on me. How the fuck could he threaten me about seeing someone else and he's fucking other bitches?

Pam turned around slowly with her eyes bucked, "Bitch, is you dumb or is you stupid? Yes, Emilio is fucking someone else. He has a wife in case you

forgot. Damn, Brynn you gone over this nigga. I ain't
ever seen you like this. Bitch you need to give that
pussy up to someone else to get that nigga off your
mind. Y'all are *not* getting married. He is *not* leaving
Onnie. Enjoy it while you can. Bitch, control the dick
don't let that dick control you. Shock was coming to
the hospital to see you. He asked me to tell you to get
in touch with him it's important. That nigga is really
feeling you. Shit, that letter may mean more than you
think. Alex said that bitch Onnie is a nut case. That
bitch may be gunning for you cuzz." She chuckled.
I had to laugh myself, "That bitch Onnie ain't built
like that. Don't get her pretty ass fucked up."

Pam laughed lightly, "Don't under estimate what
a woman will do to save her marriage. That bitch
ain't dumb you better believe it."

I grunted.

I thought about what Nash told me about her past
and how Emilio practically saved her. Onnie didn't
want to fuck with me; not even Jesus would be able
to save her ass if she was coming for me.

Chapter 21

Five days had gone by since the attack. It was the first time I went outside as well. I was supposed to meet Nash at *Firestones* on the Riverfront. He had showed up on my door step the day before. I peeked out the window but didn't answer the door. He blew my phone up so bad I had to turn it off. I wasn't in the mood to talk to anyone. My stomach stayed upset and I had a migraine out of this world. No one from my family had come to check on me. I guess Pam told them I was in my feelings. Their focus was on Amelie anyway. I did get a surprise visitor as I was leaving out.

I opened the door to leave out and was met by my long lost brother Chance. His bronze skin was glowing and his soft lips glistened from the MAC nude lip glass he was wearing. Chance was gay as shit but looking at him you couldn't tell. The hoes loved him. He had model like features with a 6'3 athletic built frame. His dress game put a lot of high fashion bitches to shame. His long wavy hair was pulled back in a ponytail. His eyebrows were arched to perfection. The camel Gucci loafers and linen suit made him look like one of those Columbian Dope dealers.

He greeted me with a tight hug. He squeezed me so hard I thought my bra was about to pop open.

"I see you heard about it." I walked back in the house and he followed behind me shutting the door.

"Thanks to the internet...yeah. Why didn't anyone think to call me? I'm family too-aren't I?" His voice was masculine yet soft. He made me feel like shit when I observed the dejected expression on his face. I would have thought Nisa would have called him. I was wrapped in my own shit I had forgot all about my brother. That was real fucked up of me.

"Damn, bro I'm sorry." I held his hand as I took a seat at the breakfast nook. I didn't want to get too comfortable because I had plans; I was going to have to make this visit short and sweet. "I was so messed up about everything that I didn't think to call you. Shit I ain't heard from or seen you in a minute." I said in my defense.

He sighed heavily. "What is that supposed to mean? I'm your brother. I should have known that my sister was almost killed. I don't understand why you or mother didn't think I should know. I was coming up this way any how because father hasn't been answering my calls for the past couple of weeks. He normally calls me twice a week to check on me and the business. I've called the office and left several messages and still no response. Do you know if he's upset with me?" Guilt ridden I blinked rapidly looking away from him. He was an emotional creature yearning for acceptance in today's society. His success did not make him exempt from phobia and prejudice that people held concerning homosexuals. That fact that our family was deep routed in the church made him extremely cautious-determined to keep his true lifestyle furtive.

Our father had made his views on same sex relations apparent on several occasions. When I went through my lesbian spell he acted as if I didn't exist for months. He had me locked away at the Rockford center for a month blaming mental illness for my behavior. There was nothing wrong with me mentally, I didn't care about anything and felt I could do whatever I wanted. I was never a lesbian my goal was to get underneath their skin and I succeeded. Chance on the other hand was truly gay. The Rockford Center would not be able to "cure" his condition this was who he chose to be.

"He knows," I mumble. I shift on the stool nervously knowing I was about to experience the ultimate Bitch fit.

He leans in towards me, "Come again?" His breathing is thick his face is now flushed.

"There was an argument I slipped up and said that Nisa was hiding that fact that you were gay."

His gaze was intense.

"Chance, you're gay and you should be proud of who you are. Why should you continue to hide it? Aren't you tired of being in the closet? I mean really this isn't back in the day there is nothing for you to be ashamed of. I dabbled in it and they still accept me." I laughed nervously hoping that he would see my point of view. "Shit you can marry a nigga now. Obama made that possible." That situation alone caused our parents who were once heavy Obama supporters to switch up and join the Republican Party.

Chance cupped his mouth in his hands and walked away from me. He placed his hands on top of his head while pacing back and forth. His jaw twitched and his eyes were red. I took a deep breath and prepared myself for the worse. Chance wasn't violent he was a cry baby. I looked at my watch I was to meet Nash in twenty minutes. Chance was going to have to say whatever was on his mind fast. I had things to do.

I inwardly sigh. "Chance, I'm…"

He turns and smiles wickedly. "You're sorry. That's what you're about to say right?"

Relieved I reply, "Yes, I am very sorry. You know I wouldn't do anything to hurt you. Shit, you, Ora and Pam are all I really have. If I could take it back I would. I was pissed and wasn't thinking. You know how I get." I laughed.

A repulsive look was thrown at me. My smile immediately faded.

"I do *know* how you get. You don't give a crap about anyone's feelings but your own. Do you know what I go through? You raped me!"

I stepped back from him. This nigga was trippin' rape though?

"Excuse me?"

"You stripped me from being able to tell my father about my life on my own terms. You snatched that from me. You do this to everyone. This is why you don't have healthy relationships. You're a lonely... *bitch* who cares about nothing but yourself. You'll never be happy. You go around and point out everyone's flaws and you are the cancer in all of our lives. I tried to take up for you for years. Amelia and mother were right you are rotten to the core. Nothing positive can come from you. I see why Lilith is resigning." Spit flew from his mouth as he spoke with rage.

"Lilith is resigning? Where did you get that idea from?" Out of all the hurtful things he said his last statement concerning Lilith was the only one that was relevant.

He cackled like the bitch he was. "Oh, you didn't know. Miss Lilith is leaving the company. I've been trying to talk her out of it for months. She's sick of you. Everyone is sick of you Brynn."

"I'm confused when did you and Lil become so chummy? Why would she confide in you?"

"There's a lot you don't know sweetheart. While you were busy screwing someone else's husband. Yes. I know all about it baby! Your bestie was making provisions to leave and take part of Fleek with her. She has that right beings as though she helped you build the company and for the last year she has been the one running it. You were busy partying and hanging with that slut cousin of yours that you had no idea what was going on. You knew that Pam was fucking Hov and you never told Lilith who was supposed to be like your sister. That was dead wrong." His mouth quirks up and he glares at me.

I stood there shaking my nerves were frazzled. For once in my life I was speechless. This was all too much for me to grasp. I had no idea that Pam was fucking Hov, now it made sense why Lilith was acting funny towards me. The thing is why would she not fuck up her husband or confront Pam. I had nothing to do with any of it. Hov didn't even have any money so why Pam would be fucking with him was a mystery to me.

My lips curled in a disdainful smile. I open my front door. "It's time for you to go."

He whips his hair and sashays past me. He turns and says through the door, "Life as you know it is about to change." He rolls his eyes and disappears to the driveway.

I slam the door. I'm enraged that he had the audacity to speak a threat to me. The fact that Pam had crossed a line that put my business in jeopardy sent me over the edge.

I peeked through my blinds to see if he was gone. I waited a few moments to make sure that he was no longer near my home. I went to the garage with my cell phone. I took several pictures of his car that I held for him. I went to my office turned on my computer and pulled up my craigslist account. I posted pictures of the vehicle and priced it for one dollar. It was nothing for me to create a title to the car. I was going to give him a lesson on what lonely rotten bitches when they are crossed.

Chapter 22

Once again I had stood Nash up. It was for good reason. My family was tripping and I had to get on top of things before they fell from underneath me. I drove up I-95 North in the pouring down rain to meet with my lawyer. After doing a little digging I realized that there was a great deal of money being snatched from my business accounts. I have new credit cards that were recently opened; there was a hundred thousand dollar loan against the company as well. Lilith had approved all of it. I checked the credit card records cash advances from the Sugar House and Harrah's casino were noted. Somebody was doing heavy gambling and I knew it wasn't Lilith. Hov had everything to do with it and when I was done with them they would be sitting underneath the bridge by the mission with the rest of the bums.

It fucked me up that Lil would do me dirty. I didn't understand why she didn't come to me concerning Pam and Hov's alleged affair. We were supposed to be better than that. I called Pam non-stop for the last couple of days. There was no answer. It didn't matter because after I left my lawyer I was going to pay her stank ass a visit. I sold Chance's car the same day I listed it. He was still in town my Aunt Ora had told me he had sat up at the hospital like the prodigal son with his phony ass family. Turns out that my father welcomed him with open arms... I was now the black sheep. I told her how Chance acted with me and the things he told me. She didn't say much. She said she had gone through it all her life with her grandmother. People didn't respect people who went against the grain and had their own mind. She told me not to worry about it and keep doing me.

She wasn't surprised when I told her about Pam. She said the bitch had a white liver and you couldn't put anything past her if dick and money was involved. I agreed. It was no secret that Pam was beyond a whore. There was no help for her. She was who she was you either was going to hate her or love her. At this point I didn't know how I felt about the bitch.

"Pam, open the door bitch I know you're in there." I banged on her door like I was the police. I had been doing this for the last twenty minutes. Two of her neighbors opened the door and stared at me like they had a problem. The look I gave them let them know not to even fuck with me. I was on my shit and they didn't want it. "Bitch I'm not leaving until you open this fucking door!" I kicked it twice and waited.

I heard the lock turn. I turned the knob and the door opened. Pam was walking in front of me with a long fuchsia bathrobe on and barefoot. Her weave was matted to the back of her head. The dishes were in her sink was piled up; empty soda cans were littered on the countertop.

There was a pungent smell of old piss lingering in the apartment. Something wasn't right. Pam had a serious case of OCD the way her apartment looked and smelled was not her at all.

"Yo, what the fuck is that smell? You pissing yourself?" I looked around her living room afraid to sit. I didn't know if that bitch was pissing on her couch or what. I checked for obvious stains before taking a seat. I sat down noticed about twenty used pregnancy test. That's where the smell was coming from. I leaned over and looked at them. They all showed positive.

Oh shit. I know this bitch ain't pregnant by Hov. This was going to be a mess. Lilith was going to lose her fucking mind when she found out. I hoped to God that Pam didn't plan on keeping it. That was too much. It was bad enough she was fucking the nigga.

"I fucked up," she croaked.
I looked at for the first time. Her complexion was pasty. She had dark rings under her eyes. She looked like she hadn't slept in days. There was white crust around her dry cracked lips. The bitch looked like she was on dippers or some shit.

"Why the fuck was you fucking that nigga in the first place. You went too far. There's some lines you just don't cross." I was stern with her like she was my child.

"Huh? What you mean why was I fucking him? You ain't say all that shit before. You thought it was cool at first. What shit ain't poppin' between you and Emilio no more?"

"I didn't know anything about you fucking Hov! Why would you think I would agree with you fucking my best friends' husband?"

"Bitch I ain't pregnant by no damn Hov! This is Alex baby. Whoever said I was fucking Hov is a motherfucking liar. I fucks with him on some business shit. I ain't fucking that nigga though. He don't even prefer pussy to tell you the truth!"

"Hold the fuck up...what you mean he don't prefer pussy?" This was some hot shit right here. I thought I had heard it all.

"Hov go both ways honey and his pop tart lame ass wife knows it. He a bonafied homo-thug. I go to the casino with him sometimes cause he be flippin' money for me on the black jack table. That nigga be trickin' with the young faggots. I guess he be usin' the money he win off the tables. Girl he takes them to Atlantic city and everything."

I was sick. I gasped. "Fuck no!"

"What!"

"Chance told me he was fucking you. He and Lilith done got all close all of a sudden. You think Chance fucking with Hov?"

Pam shrugged her shoulders. "Bitch who knows? Hov don't give a fuck about Lilith he fucking anything with legs. He said he told her that he not gonna stop doing him. If she didn't like it he would leave. He don't even be going home half the time. One night he lost big. He called her and she came all the way up Chester in the middle of the night and dropped him off four stacks. I felt so bad for her. I was at another table because I ain't want her to see me. I told him he needs to leave her alone before he give her some shit. He was like she threatened to kill herself. So he just gives her the dick and he do what he wants. It's real fucked up."

I shook my head in disbelief. Lil should have never married Hov. I knew he had shit with him. I had no idea about the gambling problem or the gay thing. I wasn't so mad at her now. She was a victim if I were a true friend I had to find a way to get her out of the mess she was in. I had to figure out what position my brother played in all this. I hope to God he wasn't fucking Hov on the low. Hov wasn't even his type. My brother was clean cut, a fly guy. Hov was nothing of the sort. My head was pounding. I picked up one of the pregnancy tests.

"Well who got you knocked and why didn't you tell me?"

"It's not a secret. Check your I.G. I been told the world when I found out two days ago." She scratched her neck. I opened my Instagram app and went to her profile. There was a picture of all the pregnancy test scattered across the table with a hashtag that read #Fuckmylyfe. She had over two hundred and fifty comments and only five likes they were all from niggas demanding her to call them.

"Really, Pam?" I dropped the test shaking my head. "You need to take this shit down you look real crazy. So you know who the father is?"

"Yes honey its Alex. I ain't been fucking nobody else. This nigga doesn't give me enough breathing room to step off with anyone else." There was disappointment all on her face.

"So did he give you money for the abortion?"

"Abortion…I wish. Soon as I posted that shit, that nigga was on my phone telling me he was on his way home. He's been here since. That's why I'm so tired. We been arguing and fucking around the clock. He said I can't have an abortion this baby is important to him."

"To him? It has to be important to you too, Pam. You and I both know you ain't the motherly type. If he doesn't give you the money, I'll help you out. You can lie and say you had a miscarriage or some shit." I couldn't let me cousin bring an innocent child in the world knowing she would fuck it up mentally.

She sighed and tilted her head back. "I can't do that. I love this dude and if he wants me to have this baby I gotta do it. He does everything for me. I can at least do this. He said he'll take care of everything. I need to chill out for a while anyway."

"How far are you?"

She shrugged her shoulders. "I don't know yet. We going to a doctor he deals with in Jersey tomorrow to find out."

I wrinkled my nose, "Why Jersey? Don't you have a GYN here you can go to?"

"He wants me to go to the doctor in Jersey. He's paying for everything I don't see what the problem is." She looked irritated.

"Does your mom know?"

"No and don't go running your mouth telling her. She'll find out when I'm ready for her to know." She snapped.

I decided to change the subject. It was her body and her situation. I just know she better not come running to me when shit backfires. Because I had a feeling Alex was going to be on some shit. He was controlling, Pam was not the type to be controlled. I hoped that he didn't end up beating her ass. That's how those island niggas were-possessive.

"Did Emilio come back with him?" I asked.

"I don't think so. I told you they went on business. Alex only came back because I was pregnant. I'll prolly see him when I go up there tomorrow. I'll tell him you're checkin' for him."

"No…don't do that I don't want to seem thirsty."

She laughed, "Bitch it's too late for that. It's no secret that you dick dumb over that nigga. Even his wife detected your thirst."

"Excuse me?"

"Alex told me that Onnie been on it since day one. That's why she trying to throw Nash your way. He says Emilio does this shit all the time but you are different."

My heart shattered in pieces. *This is something he does all the time?* I grabbed my bag I was ready to go.

"Don't look so sad cuzz. I told you Alex said you're different. That's a good thing. Maybe he'll wife you up too."

I didn't even respond. I walked out the apartment without looking back.

Chapter 23

Soft lips brush across my navel. My heart is pounding as I anticipate what is about to take place. I placed my hands on the side of his head pushing him down to where I needed him to be. He took his hands and slowly parted my knees. He gazes down at my plump shaven pussy and smile wide-eyed.

"I missed you so much," his voice is heavy filled with lust.

"I know," I murmur, and smile a wicked knowing smile.

I force his head down until I feel the heat from his breath upon my lips. He slithers his tongue in my opening and begins to nurse my clit. Soft moans escape from my lips as my body awakens from a deep slumber. I clenched my teeth together forbidding words to escape from my mouth. It had been a long time since I received a treatment from him and I was going to enjoy every bit of it.

"I love you so much," Shock lifted his head leaned over and kissed me passionately. "I want to feel you...all of you." He pleaded as he nibbled on my earlobe.

I had so many mixed feelings going on. Lilith, Chance, Pam and Emilio were draining me. I needed to get back to my old self. There was no one better to do that than my old fuck buddy Shock. Pam said he was looking for me. Although that was over a week ago, I knew he would come running if I called.

Without saying a word, I wrapped my legs firmly around his back giving him permission to have his way with me. Shock wasted no time pushing inside of me. He wasn't rough nor was he gentle. It was just right. Our bodies moved together as if we were supposed to be one. For that moment nothing else mattered but the treatment I was getting. The beautiful words that he whispered to me I could not take seriously. Too many people had betrayed me. As fine as Shock was I could never be serious with him. I was in love with Emilio as much as I didn't want to admit it. I had to find a way to get over him. So far Shock was doing a good job. A few more sessions with him and I should be back to myself.

Shock blew my back out for hours. After he was finished he rolled off me. He was on his knees looking down at his dick. I sat up in the bed and looked down.

"Fuck outta here!" I yelled. I fell back on the bed. I had a headache all over again. The condom was torn to shreds. The first go around I sucked his ass dry. When we went for the rest of the rounds I made him use a condom because my jaws was sore. I wasn't sucking his dick like a champ round for round. I wasn't built like that.

"I'm sorry I didn't know. You were so wet I couldn't tell it broke." He said in his defense. "I'm sorry babe." He squeezed my thigh. I moved away and ran to the bathroom. I grabbed a box of Summers Eve out of the cabinet stood over the toilet and douched immediately. I didn't want none of his babies swimming up my canal. That's all I needed. After I was finished I went back in the bedroom Shock was sitting on the side of the bed with his head down.

I lay back in the bed. "What time are you leaving?"
He turned around. "Huh?" he had a puzzled look on his face.

"When are you leaving? It's almost midnight shouldn't you be getting back on the road?"
He stood up and his hard dick was slowly going down. It was appetizing but I was done for the night. That broken condom shit fucked up my mental.

"Are you serious?" he asked.

"I'm sleepy, Shock. Shit we been fucking for the last five hours. I got shit to do in the morning. I'll call you later this week. We can go out to dinner or something. Just make sure you buy me something nice to wear. You know what I like." I winked and smiled seductively.

He stood there like he was in a state of confusion.

"Brynn, I love you. Didn't you hear me say that?"

"Yeah, and you was in my pussy when you said it. A lot of niggas say shit they don't mean when they're in a nice fat wet box."

"I'm not a lot of niggas. I love you. I've been trying to make you my wife for years and you don't know how far I'll go for you. I'll do anything for you Brynn. I helped your family. The cops was trying to pin that shit on me and I went through all that on the strength of you. Why can't you see that? I can have any bitch out here. Especially, your THOT ass cousin Pam. That bitch tries to throw the pussy at me every chance she gets. I turn her down because I don't want no one but you."

It all sound good to me. I wanted to believe him but I my mind wouldn't allow it.

"Nigga, I ain't trying to hear that shit. You way in Atlantic City half the time. You not gonna sit here and make me believe your sexy ass ain't fucking no bitches. If you ain't then your ass must be gay."

He jumped on the bed and pinned me down. His eyes were dark, his nose flared and for the first time I felt fear.

"Don't you ever say no crazy shit like that to me again! I love you. I don't want nobody else but you. I will do anything for you don't you see that?"

I could feel his heart beating rapidly. I was having an adrenaline rush of my own. I couldn't lie I was turned on.

"Would you do anything for me?" I whispered.

"I already have," He forced his tongue in my mouth and I kissed him back.

Chapter 24

"Long time no see," Nash sat down at the booth facing me. We were at Onnie's restaurant in the mall. Three weeks had passed since the murder. I hadn't seen anyone except Pam, Shock and now Nash. I hadn't heard from anyone in my immediate family since Chance left my house. I didn't go to Felito's funeral. No one had called to see if I was coming anyway. I was officially an outcast. I thought I would at least have heard from my father. The only one who checked on me daily was Aunt Ora. I hadn't even heard from Pam. I called the day she was supposed to find out how far she was but the phone went straight to voicemail. I tried a few days later and it did the same thing. I figured she was busy boo lovin' with her new baby daddy.

Shock had stayed with me for the last two weeks. It was awkward. I was afraid that Emilio would come through the door at any moment-he didn't. It was a good thing because I'm sure Shock would have stood up to him. They were both powerful men in their own right. I didn't want them beefin' over me. Shock had left to check on his business. He assured me that he would be back that Sunday. I was happy he was leaving this would give me time to think. The shit he was saying to me was unreal. Emilio talked the same way about doing anything for me and killing a motherfucker. Although Shock never mentioned killing his obsession over me lead me to believe he would do it.

I texted Nash because he would send me messages daily. He didn't have to check on me; it was only right that I gave him some time.

"You look fine in that peach and white," I complimented his outfit. The color scheme blended well with his complexion.

"You look beautiful yourself - a little tired but still beautiful."
My smile was weak. I hadn't been feeling well at all. I was totally stressed out from all the shit that was going on with me and my weird ass relationships.

"Yeah, I have a lot going on. My partner and I are splitting up. So I've been meeting with lawyers and trying to get my office together. Things haven't been that great with my family since the murder."

"What's that about?"

"I don't know. I didn't get along with my brother in-law. My cousin Pam and I were actually in a fight with him. I caught him cheating on my sister at the bar. When I confronted him it got ugly fast."

"Did your sister appreciate it?"

"No, she resented me for it. It caused a blow up at the family dinner and we stopped speaking. The day of our picnic I went over to apologize and that's when I found out he was dead and she was beaten."

"So you never got to make peace with them."

"Nope, it got worse when I went to the hospital. My mother had the balls to say she thought I had something to do with it. I would never have someone hurt my sister."

"What about her husband?"

"No comment," I laughed.

He smiled. "Why didn't you call me sooner? I could have helped you through some of this." He placed his hands on mine. They were soft and strong.

"I had to handle this on my own. My family is a difficult monster. I would never subject anyone to them. The only one I can stomach is my Aunt Ora and sometimes Pam."

"Pam, as in Alex's friend Pam." He said.

"I think she's more than his friend, try his new baby mama." I laughed.

He stared at me straight faced.

"Don't tell me you didn't know."

"I don't get into his business. I didn't think Pam was anything more than a friend. Now you tell me she is having a baby by him. He's full of surprises." He chuckled and opened the menu.

Now he had me wondering what was really up with Alex.

"Is Alex involved with anyone besides Pam? I don't know how when he's with her all the time and he's forcing her to have this baby."

He raised eyebrow. "*Forcing* her to have the baby?"

"Yes, he told her abortion wasn't an option. He's even setting up doctors' appointments." I informed him. He wasn't going to act like my cousin was some side chick giddy to have this niggas baby.

"Alex is a very married man. He has several wives. I didn't think Pam was the type to go for that sort of thing."

I choked on my water. I coughed and he hurried to my side to make sure I was ok.

"I'm good…what the fuck you mean by several wives. What this nigga Muslim? We don't do the *Big Love* thing on this side of the Atlantic." He must have had us fucked up. Pam wasn't going for any bullshit like that. At least she better not had. My mind was racing. Maybe that's why her ass had been ducking me. I was going to find out. "Look Nash, I'm a have to get up with you later. I need to handle something."

He stood up ready to say something. I kissed him softly on the lips to shut him up. Onnie had walked up on us when she saw me kiss him she smiled. Out the corner of my eye I saw Emilio standing by the kitchen door. I hurried and turned away from him. I secretly wished that he had seen me kiss Nash. That nigga needed to know I wasn't going to sit around and wait like a sick puppy while he did disappearing acts for weeks.

***

I was back banging on Pam's door once again. She wasn't answering and I didn't see her car in the garage. That didn't mean anything. She was good for hiding her shit to avoid company. I knocked and dialed her number back to back. After fifteen minutes her neighbor opened the door. He was a tall blonde, reminded me of a Hollister model. All he was missing was a surfboard and beach shorts.

"She doesn't reside there anymore."

"What do you mean? She does still live here you don't know what you're talking about."

"No actually you don't know what *you're* talking about." He retorted. "She moved out last Tuesday night. The Rasta dude let us raid the apartment. She didn't take much with her. She left in a hurry. She's not on the run or involved in that gangster stuff is she?" His eyes widened in amusement. I still didn't believe him.

"Come look she gave me those cool lamps."

I went over to his apartment and sure enough he had her lamps and a few paintings.

I ran out and got into my car to call my Aunt Ora. I dialed her number and there was a tap at my window. I turned to see who it was and froze. It was Emilio.

Chapter 25

"You take me for a joke don't you?"
I sat quietly on my bed watching him walk back and forth. He followed me home after leaving Pam's. I didn't get a chance to talk to my Aunt. I needed to know what was up with my cousin. I wasn't in the mood for his shit. I figured that the sooner I dealt with him. I would be able to move on with what was really important.

"I was thinking the same thing. You fuck me and then vanish for two weeks. You don't call to see if I'm living or dead. Oh I forgot I'm not your wife. I'm just some bitch who you fuck." I was tired of playing games with him. He was on some other shit-him and Alex both. I wasn't for it.

He grabbed my face and squeezed it tightly. I swung out of habit.

"Get the fuck off me!" I shouted.

He squeezed harder and started to unbuckle his pants. I swung harder but I was no match for him he was faster and stronger. He moved his body on top of mine and snatched my pants down. I continued to fight until I grew weak. By then he was already inside of me grunting and confessing his love for me. I wasn't feeling it at all. Normally I would enjoy it. I wanted him off of me. But my body did not agree. I was having orgasm after orgasm which made him go harder. I wanted to cry but that wasn't going to do any good. He would have thought it was cries of passion. Nash came to my mind I wish he was here to save me.

Emilio stayed the night with me. The next morning, he got up like everything was normal. I woke up sick as a dog. I threw up so much that stomach acid was coming out. I stayed in the bed the entire day while he made himself at home. He brought food for me to eat the smell of it made me sick. I managed to text my Aunt Ora. She told me she knew that Pam had moved she thought I knew. I asked her did she know where Pam moved too and she stated she did not know. I wanted to tell her about the pregnancy so bad but I didn't want her to be mad at me.

Later that evening I was just waking up from a nap. Emilio was lying next to me ass naked. As soon as he saw my eyes open he was guiding my head to his dick.

"I can't I don't feel good."

"This will make you feel better." He said.

I snatched away from him.

"I want you to go home."

He laughed. "I am home."

"If you don't leave I'm going to tell your wife." I threatened.

He sat up and smiled. "She already knows." He handed me his phone. "Call her."

I thought he was bluffing. I took the phone from him and looked for her number and called her. The phone rang twice and she answered it.

"Emilio are you coming home?"

My heart stopped. I opened my mouth but nothing came out.

"Hello…"

Silence.

She took a deep breath and whispered, "Brynn is that you? Text me your number it's important that we talk. You are in danger…" I swallowed hard. Emilio noticed the frightened look on my face. He snatched the phone from me.

"Hello," he said. She must have hung. "She's trying to push Nash on you to keep you away from me. I told her to stop if she wants her brother to live. That goes for anyone. You're mine. Now come suck my dick." He grabbed my head and I did as he requested.

***

The next day I woke up throwing up again. I felt and looked like shit. Emilio suggested that I get dressed because he wanted to take me out somewhere. I knew there was no use of arguing with him. Onnie said I was in danger. I wasn't sure if that was some bullshit but the way she was acting she was most likely telling the truth. I took a shower and put on a bright pink Maxi dress that I picked up from Express. I had never worn it I decided to put it to use. I pulled my hair back in a tight ponytail applied lip gloss and bronzer. My face was losing its vibrancy. I grabbed my Tory Burch Satchel bag from my closet and threw my wallet inside. I put on my Prada shades and headed to the door. Emilio was standing by the window talking on the phone. I walked passed him. He grabbed my arm. "Do you know him?"

I looked out the window and it was Shock. *Fuck my life.* I was not ready for this to go down. I shook my head no and went out the door. I texted Shock and told him to act like he didn't know me. I turned my phone off before he could respond. I stood on the passenger side and watched Shock get out of the car. *Oh shit. Please no.* Emilio walked out the house and locked the door keeping his eyes on Shock the entire time. I put my head down. Shock went to the house next door and rang the doorbell. Emilio unlocked the door and I jumped in the car. Emilio took his time getting in and started the car. Shock was watching us out the side of his eye. I saw him reach for his cell phone and Emilio pulled off.

We arrived at Onnie's restaurant and my stomach started to turn again. Not because I was nervous. The smell made me ill. He held my hand as we walked in the place. All eyes were on us. Onnie greeted her husband and kissed him on the lips as if it were nothing. She turned her attention to me. "Can I get you anything, Brynn." Her voice let me know she was uncomfortable.

"I would like a bottle of water." I dare not ask for water in a cup that bitch might have spit it in it. She didn't have to worry about me eating in there ever again. I sat down at a table in the corner far away from everyone. Alex walked in alone. I wanted to ask him about Pam but I dare not move. He and Emilio went to the back in the kitchen area. Onnie came in and handed me the bottled water.

"Why didn't you text me?" She whispered.
Before I could answer Alex and Emilio came back out. They both had perplexed looks on their face. Emilio came over to us. "Onnie I need you to take her home now." I will see you both in a few days something came up." He looked to Onnie. "Is my passport in the same place?"
She nodded.

Once he was gone she went to the back. She came out with her purse in hand. "Let's go!"

Chapter 26

"Where are you taking me?" I asked. We were driving down route one headed towards Kent County.

"Brynn, I never formally introduced myself to you."

I was confused. "What?"

"I don't know what Nash told you but there is so much more to me than you can imagine. We didn't grow up in New Jersey like I'm sure he told you. We lived in a nice neighborhood in Montgomery County, Pennsylvania. My mother was Cuban. She was beautiful on the outside, her insides were dreadful. She was in the hair business, like you. She owned a salon. It wasn't upscale but she kept it nice. We lived in a single family home in a diverse neighborhood. I had an older sister that was under Nash. Her name was Drusella. Our father was from Mexico he had an old garage where he worked on cars. It was located in Philadelphia. My father appeared to be a hard man but he was gentle. My mother was the problem. She was a glamour girl. She was the Cuban Farrah Fawcett. She wore vintage clothes by Gucci and other designers while my sister and I wore rags. She took us to the second hand store to get clothing. She said she wanted us to learn that we had to earn what we needed. She would tell us that she worked hard to get her salon and was able to afford the fabrics she wore because she was self-made, not put on like a basic gold digger whore.

Our home appeared to be immaculate. We had electronic blinds, crown molding, everything was lily white. It was perfect. We had to keep the house scrubbed not a crumb could be on the floor. It was so clean that you could eat from the floor. There was only one issue. At night when the blinds closed and the lights went out. It was raining roaches."

I cringed at the thought. "How was the house that clean and you had that many roaches?" That shit didn't make sense to me.

"I used to ask myself the same thing. We were on section 8. No one knew it. Looking at my mother you would have thought she had a secret life. She would throw extravagant parties. My father would protest but she would kick him out. He wasn't welcomed in his own home. The only comfort he received was from Drusella and me. She treated us the same way. Not Nash, he was a boy so he was her golden child. She would bring food home and give it to him. Dru and I would get the left over pieces. Sometimes it would be a piece of biscuit and chicken crisp. We had to share it. My mother didn't like the attention that my dad gave us. So one day he left for work and we never seen daddy again. It got worse.

Nash was being treated like the king and we were the servants. She would buy one box of maxi pads for us to share. When we ran out we would use the brown shampoo towels from her salon. We had to wash them and re-use them until she decided to buy us more pads.

I remember having to put card board in my shoes and crazy glue it to the sole. My sister Dru grew tired of her; she started to steal her clothes and would wear them to school. When she found out she beat both of us with a cable cord.

"Did Nash know this was happening?" I had to ask because this didn't sound anything like the story he told me.

"Of course he did, He turned a blind eye to it because he was the apple of my mother's eye and he did no wrong. Why would he go against her to suffer our fate? My mother took us to see a friend of hers named Filipe in New Jersey. He didn't live far from our grandmother. He had a son named Emil. He was only a few years older than Nash. Filipe was very nice to us. Real nice. He suggested that we live with my grandmother. He gave my mother a large amount of amount of money. Before my mother left she talked to Dru alone. It turned out that I was the only one going with my grandmother. Drusella went to live with Filipe. I didn't see Dru again for months when I did she looked fabulous but she had a big belly. She was only sixteen and she was pregnant. When I asked her about it she said I was too young to understand. The next year Nash came to live with us because my mother had died of a drug over dose. He became good friends with Emil. During that time I had turned fifteen and Emil showed interest in me."

"Emil is Emilio?" I asked.

She shook her head yes. "Nash went into the service and I became Emil's girl. It wasn't long before I had a big belly myself." Her voice became weak.

"You have a child?" I was stunned I had no idea that Onnie had children.

A tear dropped from her eye. "I had eleven children."

There was silence between us for a good ten minutes. How the fuck did she have eleven kids? Where were they? Nash didn't say shit about having any nieces or nephews. Did she lose them all? I had so many questions but was afraid to ask.

"Where are your kids now Onnie?"

She pulled over in the Wal-Mart parking lot. There were snot and tears running down her face. I gave her a tissue from my bag.

She turned to me slowly shaking her head. "They're gone…" she cried.

My heart dropped. She must have had an Omen on her. How did all of her kids die?

"I'm sorry were they still born? Crib death?"

"No they are all gone. Emilio sold them."

That fucked me up. I felt the vomit come up in my throat.

"Sold them? Bitch you are lying." I said through clenched teeth. There was no way she was going to make me believe that shit. Who sells babies? That was some shit you seen on Lifetime movie. Only white people did that shit in real life.

"I swear to you. Why would I lie about something like that? That is what Emilio does. His father Filipe did the same thing to my sister. She couldn't take it anymore. After the fifth baby she killed herself. Emilio told me when I asked where she was. Alex does the same thing. They find young girls who are either pregnant and buy the babies or they do it themselves. Alex has six women who live at the big house. They all have babies. Emilio only married me to keep me quiet and our babies were worth more because they were beautiful. It's sick people out here and a lot of desperate people who can't have babies. He covers it up as an adoption agency. It's been in his family for years. Your cousin Pam is in New Jersey with them. I don't think you'll ever see her again."

"Pam would not go for that!"

"She has no choice. If they think she will be a threat they will kill her."

I couldn't hold it back any longer. I screamed punched the dashboard. What the fuck did I get myself in to? I looked at Onnie and wanted to punch her in the face. She should have been told me.

"Does Nash know?"

"No, he never knew I was pregnant…ever. He's waiting for me to have a baby."

"Why didn't he mention his sister to me?"

"Nash has guilt. He thinks she killed herself because our mother gave her away. He never spoke of her again it's like she didn't exist."

"Why are you telling me this?"

"Because your next, Brynn. Emilio wants you for himself."

"What! I'm not having any babies and the hell if I would give them up."

She shook her head and threw it back. "It's too late. He knows you're pregnant. He told me. He served me divorce papers last week."

My head began to spin. There was no way I was pregnant and if I was it wasn't a guarantee it was his. I had been sick but I just didn't want to face it.

"If I'm pregnant it may not be his." I whispered.

Onnie reached over and hugged me. "I pray that it is. If it's not God have mercy on our soul."

"What do you mean?"

"I was supposed to report to him if I saw you with anyone. I tried to push you to Nash because I know he wouldn't hurt my brother and leave you alone. If you are pregnant and it's not his you will be treated like the others or even killed."

"Do you think that he had anything to do with Felito?"

"I thought so at first but he thought it was me. He was with Alex the entire time. I don't know who did that. I do know this. If you want to survive this we have to work together."

***

Onnie dropped me off in front of my house and my father's car was parked out front.

"Who's that?" she asked.

"It's just my father. I will call you later tonight so we can figure this out."

I got out the car and headed towards the door. I walked by him like I didn't see him in the car. I unlocked my door and left it open. I threw my pocketbook on the counter grabbed the remote and went to the bar to fix myself a drink. I felt like I was trapped in a segment of the Twilight Zone. I heard the front door shut and took a deep breath. Daddy walked in slowly pulled up his pants at the knee and sat in the recliner chair. I turned the television on and started to flick through the channels. I tried to stay calm. It was hard after hearing that my love was a fucking psycho path.

"Why haven't you answered your phone?" His tone was stern.

"I turned it off."

"Turn the television off we need to talk."

"I have nothing to talk to you about." I turned on BET Baby Boy was on. I turned the volume up took the shot of Remy to the head and continued to ignore him.

"I'm not going to ask you again. Turn the television off." He raised his voice.
I turned it up to the max. After all the shit I went through he was not going to come in here demanding shit from me.

I heard him grunt as he got up from the chair. I was hoping he was leaving instead he ripped the television from my wall and threw it to the floor. The screen cracked and blacked out.

"Are you fucking crazy? Do you know how much that fucking television cost!"
He reared his hand back and slapped me across my face. He hit me so hard I thought my head was about to disconnect from my shoulders. I sat there holding my face. I was afraid to say a word. My father hadn't hit me since I was in first grade.

"Now you listen to me! Your Brother is missing, Lilith and Ravon are dead! They found another one of those letters. Now you tell me what the hell is going on! Laurie is losing her mind. She told me that you and Lilith had a falling out. What do you have to do with this?"

He was lying. There was no way that they were all dead. Someone was framing me and I wanted to know why!

"I don't believe you! You're just saying this!"
He pulled the envelope from his pocket and threw it at me. It had the same black lip imprints from before.

I won't stop until she stops...

The same thing that was on the other letter, what the fuck did that mean?

"How did you get this?" I asked.

"Laurie found it on Lilith's body."

"Oh God! How did they die?" I cried.

He sat down and shook his head. "They were all in the bedroom. Chance and Ravon...they...they were performing a sexual act while Lilith recording it." He got choked up and started to cry.

I turned to the side and vomited on the floor. The thought of them in my mind made me ill. I laid over the edge and cried. I felt like the walls were closing in on me. I wanted to die. Who could I trust? Maybe it would be better if I was gone. My life had gone from sugar to shit in less than a year. Was God punishing me for my wicked ways? I was really in a bad episode of the *Twilight Zone*. Shit like this didn't happen in real life. There was a knock at my door. I couldn't move. I didn't have enough strength to tell them to come in. There was another knock and my father got up to open the door.

"Brynn, this young man is here to see you." I turned to see who it was and it was Shock. I reached out for him and he came to me without hesitation.

"Baby, I heard what happened. Are you ok?"
I cried in his arms.

"I have to get back home with your mother." My dad looked at Shock. "Take care of my daughter and bring her over to our home tonight. She needs to be with family."

"Yes, sir." Shock said.

The door shut and looked up at him. "I need to get away from here. I'm in trouble."

"What do you mean?" he said.

"I'm pregnant and it's yours." I said.

He smiled.

"Are you sure?"

"I'm positive but that man that you saw here earlier. He is going to hurt me if he finds out that I'm with you. He said he'll kill anyone that gets in his way. He's going to hurt me and I need you! I have to get out of here!"

Shock held me in his arms. "I told you I will take care of everything. No one is going to hurt you. Especially now since you are carrying my seed."

"You promise?" I asked.

"I put that on my life…"

It was nine thirty in the evening I had packed a few bags while Shock changed the locks on all my doors. I had to get the fuck out of dodge until I could figure out what to do. I didn't trust Onnie as far as I could throw her. She had a hidden agenda and that was to save her raggedy ass. The story she told me about her mother was fucked up. That bitch was worse than Faye Dunaway in *Mommy Dearest*. I knew people who grew up in the projects who ain't have it as bad as her. Although I felt bad for her, I was not about to let that nigga Emilio wife me up. He was breeding baby makers. The hell if he was going to have me knocked the fuck up so he can sell something that came from my pussy. There was not enough money in the world.

Onnie knew that shit was wrong. I found fault with her because she was so in love with money that she let the shit go on. The problem was her ass done got old and that womb was worn out. She could save those tears for the next bitch. If my cousin Pam was stupid enough to go along with it fuck her too. It's funny how quick your regard for someone changes when your very own life was on the line. I loved my brother to death. Only God knew where he was and I prayed he was safe. But the life he was into was fucked up. The only person besides him I truly grieved for was Lilith. She was a sweet soul. My heart hurt thinking about it. *Damn bitch why didn't you just leave his ass!* I know running would make me look guilty but I was going to have to eat that. There was no way I was going to sit back and wait for Emilio to come back and snatch my ass up.

"I'm ready," I ran down the steps with my bags. When I reached the end of the steps I dropped them. "What are you doing here?" It was Nash. He was standing in the middle of the floor sizing up Shock.

"Brynn, what's going on?" He asked.

I picked up my bags and handed them to Shock, "Put these in your car."

"You good?" he asked mean mugging Nash.

"Yeah, give me a minute." He left out the door.

"Look Nash I don't know what the fuck is up with your family but I'm not going to be caught up in this shit. Your sister is fucking crazy she told me the *truth* about everything!"

"What do you mean? I told you everything."

"You left out one little detail…Drusella."

He came towards me. "What did you say?" I backed away. "Drusella, the sister your mother sold to be Filipe, Emilio's father. She killed herself because of what they made her do!" I shouted.

"You don't know what you're talking about," His tone was threatening.

"I know exactly what I'm talking about. Your sister is sick! She let Emilio get rid of her children!"

"What! Onnie never had kids! What the fuck are you talking about?"

"Ask Onnie about the eleven kids her husband sold. Ask her about the divorce papers. She only wanted you to be with me because she wants to keep her husband!"

I tried to walk past him and he grabbed my arm. "Get off of me!" I screamed. Shock came running in and hopped on Nash. They tussled and I tried to break it up. Shock was getting with him but I knew Nash was in the army. He could kill Shock without thinking twice. "Let's go! Stop it!" They weren't letting go of each other. So I grabbed my lamp and clocked Nash on the side of his head. He fell to the side and we both headed to the door when I got outside there were two state police cars speeding up to my yard with flashing lights.

Fuck!

An unmarked car pulled up on my driveway. The detective that handled my sisters' case got out the car flashing his badge, "Brynn Davis. I need you to come with me to the station to answer a few questions concerning the disappearance of your brother Chance Davis, and the murder of your business partner Lilith and her husband." I dropped my head and followed him to the car. I knew shit was about to get hectic. If they went in that house and saw Nash bleeding on the floor I was a goner....

Chapter 27

I sat in Troop two for three hours being questioned about the murders. I sat in most uncomfortable metal chair at a cold steel table sipping a bottle of hot no frills water. My bladder was about to bust but I refused to sit my ass on their filthy ass toilet. The people they had running in and out of there looked like they had Ebola or some other horrid disease. They had me in small ass room like I was on the *First 48hrs* unlike the individuals they had on the show I wasn't singing like a bird for a weak ass cup of coffee and stale cigarette. I detested that show they should change the name to *Snitches*. They were some of the sorriest criminals in the world.

I don't know what was taking Shock so long to come get me. They didn't take him only me. I thank God they didn't go inside the house my ass would have been booked for real. I hoped Nash was ok. I was sketchy about his ass but I didn't want the nigga

170

to bleed out, especially in my house. I had to get on the road I had no idea when Emilio was going to pop back up. Too much shit was going on my brother was missing and best friend was dead. The way they died was on some lifetime movie type shit. Everything around me was turning into a motion picture. My cousin caught up in some black market baby scam. My head was pounding. "This can't be life." I said out loud.

The door swung open and a light skin broad with an ancient Halle Berry hair cut came through the door with a thick brown file under arm.

"Here we go…" I rolled my eyes when she sat in front of me.

She smiled.

That shit was fake a hell.

"Ms. Davis, I'm Agent Natalia Sullivan." Her voice was heavy with a thick country accent. She was petite, cute yet had no sense of style. The navy three piece suit and nude stockings made me think of Jodi Foster in *Silence of the Lambs*. She was in need of a personal stylist and the entire line of Fleek' hair products. I noticed the one carat diamond ring on her finger. She had a band that matched. I was surprised to see that she was married. I wondered if he was as out of touch with fashion as she was. He was probably some bama as Negro she went to high school with.

"Look, I don't know anything about my brother's whereabouts or the murder. I have no idea why I'm even here. I'm tired. I need to use the restroom. I'm uncomfortable. I do believe if you're not charging me with anything I should be let go. That is the law-right Ms. F.B.I.?"

She smiled again and opened up the folder. She began to place pictures on the table. One was of a huge plantation styled home. It was beautiful. I was privy to nice places but this was straight out of a magazine. I looked at the rest and noticed a familiar face...mine.

"Hold up! What's this about?" It was a picture of Emilio and me leaving the gym. There were several pictures of him, Onnie, Alex, Nash and a few other people I had never seen. "I don't know what's this is about but I have nothing to do with it."
My stomach was doing somersaults.
She sat back in her chair. She pulled out another folder from underneath the big file.

"Do you know him?" she held up a picture of Shock.

"Yeah, Shock that's my child's father. What about him?"

Her eyebrow raised and she grunted. "Are you sure about that?"

"Am I sure about what?" My tone escalated.

"Are you sure that Darien Butler is your child's father?"

Now I was confused. "Who the hell is Darien? I said Shock..." She held her hand up and pushed four documents in front of my face.

It was four separate ID's with different names, Baron Jones for New Jersey, Andre Johnson for Georgia, Larry Smith for Connecticut and Darien Butler for Arizona. All of the identification cards had Shock's picture on them.

"Darien is wanted in four states two for kidnapping, murder, stalking and drug trafficking."
She showed me the evidence to support her accusations. I almost fell out of my chair. This couldn't be right. I was about to leave town with this nigga.

"Does this look familiar?" She showed me a plastic bag with envelopes with black kisses for a seal. "Mr. Butler stalked family members of these women and killed them when they broke off communication with him. This man has been in and out of mental institutes since he was a child. He has been on the run for five years now. We were working the Fuentes case when we stumbled across him. It seems to be you have a thing for criminals. After looking at your record we see that you aren't on the straight and narrow yourself."

I held my tongue. I was about to tell her where the hell she could go but my mind was too fucked up and who knows what would have slipped from my lips.

"Darien killed your brother in law, attacked your sister, he's responsible for the possible murder of your brother and murder of your friends. You were about to skip town with this murderer. Once he found out that the baby you are caring is not his but Mr. Fuentes, what do you think he was going to do with you?"

"How do you know this is not his baby?"
She smiled again and stood up. She folded her boney arms across her flat chest and began to walk in circles around me.

"There's not too much we don't know. See we've been following Emilio and his operation for over a year. His wife, Onnie has been working with us for the past six months to gain immunity. She told us about you. She was afraid that he was going to make you his next victim and she was right."

I jumped to my feet. "You mean to tell me that you allowed him to impregnate me so he can sell our child. That shit ain't legal!"

"Have a seat Ms. Davis." She pulled my chair out and grilled me.
This frail bitch was lucky she had a badge or I would have trashed her.

"You became a part of our investigation. We were going to make an arrest once your cousin Pam went to the main house. However, the murders kept happening. You were in the middle of everything so we had to watch everything to make sure nothing messed up our arrest. Now that we have Darien in custody we can focus on Emilio. You are a victim in more ways than one rather people may agree with it or not."

I folded my arms.

174

"What do you mean if people agree or not?"

"You were involved with a married man and the jury may not look at you as a victim since you were having a mutual affair. The jury may not agree that you were impregnated against your will like the others. If they look at these pictures you two seem to be in love. However, when you look at these you seem to have a thing for Nash as well, not to mention Darien who you've been with for years. Maybe it's not a good idea for you to go on the stand. Your character is shot despite how successful you are."

"You don't know shit about me!" I shouted. I couldn't believe she had the nerve to judge me. I loved Dick and yes I'd done some dumb shit for the love of it but who hadn't.

"I'm not here to judge you or make you feel bad. I wanted to let you know that you can file charges against Mr. Fuentes for your condition. Darien or Shock as you call him will be charged for the murders and you're free to go." She picked up the files and turned to leave.

"What's going to happen to Emilio?"

"As we speak they are raiding that home I showed you. We have Alex in custody the women and children will be taken to local hospitals to be checked out...your cousin Pam included. The only one missing is Mr. Fuentes.

I was relieved Pam was safe.

Agent Sullivan, put her hand on the door. She turned to me and said, "Brynn your choices have hurt not only you but those around you. You lost a best friend and brother and now you're bringing a child that you and I both know that you really don't want in the world. I hope that you take this experience and make the right decisions for yourself and those connected to you…especially that baby. I wish you well."

She exited the room.

I didn't go home. I called a cab and had them take me to the Embassy Suite in Newark. I took a hot shower and thought about my life. I was a fucked up individual. There was no way I could bring a baby into this world. I was selfish and my selfishness brought death to my door step. Somewhere in my ill mind I I looked at love as a game. I fought so hard to avoid love that I allowed myself to fall in love not with Emilio-I fell in love with his representative. I hadn't a clue who he really was. I always told people to be themselves and truth be told, I had no idea who the hell I was…

Epilogue...

Dallas, Texas four years later

"Oh my goodness look how big she's gotten." I placed my hand on his shoulder as I looked into the computer screen.

Aubrey smiled and showed us a collage she made in her pre-school class. There was a picture of her family.

"Who is that?" he asked pointing to a picture of me she decorated with purple hearts.

Aubrey's face brightened when he asked. "That's my birth mom, my Auntie Brynn."

Footsteps could be heard coming in her direction she turned around and squealed, "Mommy!" she raised her hands for Onnie to pick her up.

Nash and I laughed.

"She's too big for you to be picking up she's a big girl now." Nash said.

"She'll always be my baby." Onnie kissed her chunky cheeks.

"Tell him Onnie...you can hold her as much as you want. I know I'm going to spoil him." I said rubbing my belly.

Onnie laughed, "I know that's right. I can't wait to meet my nephew."

"Three more months and he'll be here." I said.

"Well guys we have to go Aubrey has dance class and we don't want to be late. Blow your kisses baby."

Aubrey and Onnie blew us kisses and we disconnected.

Several months after the raid my brothers' body was found floating in the Delaware River they said he had died of a drug overdose and someone must have tossed him in. I never believed it. Emilio was never caught but I never heard from him again. Onnie and I were put into the Witness Protection program and given a new chance on life. I had to walk away from everything that I built and the ones I loved. It was a bittersweet situation. I was able to keep my life, yet I was losing it at the same time. Nash appeared at my new residence when I was eight months pregnant. He was back with the military and was able to pull a few strings to get to be reunited with me.

After I gave birth to Aubrey I did a legal adoption with Onnie. Nash and I had discussed it when I was eight months pregnant. I wasn't ready to be a mother I had too much soul searching to do. I gave her to someone I knew would treat her right. I wanted to go to Darien's trial. Everything in me wanted to let him know how I felt about him. He deceived me in the worse way. I heard Pam turned out to be a great mother but she was still Pam. I loved my family but we would never be the same and they didn't understand me or my decisions. I had to live my life for me.

Nash and I married, two years after I gave birth. I went back to school for Behavioral Science. I was now a therapist at a Domestic Violence Shelter. Life was nothing like I had imagined it to be. It was more meaningful. I had a reason to live...

The End

So Real You Feel You've Lived It!

Street Knowledge Publishing LLC
1902-B Maryland Ave
Wilmington, DE 19805
TOLL FREE: **1.888.401.1114**
www.streetknowledgepublishing.com

Date: _____

Purchaser _____
Mailing Address _____
City _____ State _____ Zip Code _____

Qty.	ISB Number	Title of Book	Price Each	Total
	978-0-9822515-6-0	Bloody Money	$15.00	
	978-0-9822515-9-1	Bloody Money 2	$15.00	
	978-0-9799556-4-8	Bloody Money 3	$15.00	
	978-0-9799556-0-0	Tommy Good story	$15.00	
	978-0-9822515-0-8	Tommy Good Story II	$15.00	
	978-0-9746199-1-0	Me & My Girls	$15.00	
	978-0-9746199-0-3	Cash Ave	$15.00	
	978-0-9822515-1-5	Merry F$$kin' Xmas	$15.00	
	978-0-9799556-0-7	A Day After Forever	$15.00	
	978-0-9822515-3-9	A Day After Forever 2	$15.00	
	978-0-9746199-6-5	Don't Mix the Bitter with the Sweet	$15.00	
	978-0-9799556-9-3	Playing For Keeps	$15.00	
	978-0-9799556-3-1	Pain Freak	$15.00	
	978-0-9799556-5-5	Dipped Up	$15.00	
	978-0-9799556-6-2	No Love No Pain	$15.00	
	978-0-9746199-4-1	Dopesick	$15.00	
	978-0-9799556-7-9	Lust, Love & Lies	$15.00	
	978-0-9746199-7-2	The Queen of New York	$15.00	
	978-0-9746199-8-9	Sin 4 Life	$15.00	
	978-0-9822515-4-6	A Little More Sin	$15.00	
	978-0-9746199-5-8	The Hunger	$15.00	
	978-0-9746199-3-4	Money Grip	$15.00	
	978-0-9822515-7-7	Young Rich and Dangerous	$15.00	
	978-1-944151-26-3	Street Victims	$15.00	
	978-1-944151-28-7	Street Victims II	$15.00	
	978-1-944151-30-3	Street Victimes III	$15.00	
	978-1-944151-32-4	A Small Wonder	$15.00	
	978-1-944151-45-4	Coup De Grace	$15.00	
	978-1-944151-47-8	Burton Boys (May 2017)	$15.00	
	978-1-944151-56-0	Burton Boys 2	$15.00	
	978-1-944151-58-4	Burton Boys 3	$15.00	
	978-1-944151-00-3	Dirty Living	$15.00	
	978-1-944151-65-2	Watch What You Say	$15.00	
		Total Books Ordered	Quantity	
			Subtotal	

SHIPPING/HANDLING (Via U.S. Priority Mail)
$7.20 for 1st book, $2.00 for each additional book
Institutional Check & Money Orders ONLY
(No Personal Checks Accepted)

	Shipping
	Total

Total | $

Street Knowledge Publishing LLC
1902-B Maryland Ave
Wilmington, DE 19805
TOLL FREE: **1.888.401.1114**
www.streetknowledgepublishing.com

Date: _____

Purchaser _____

Mailing Address _____

City _____ State _____ Zip Code _____

Qty.	ISB Number	Title of Book	Author	Price Each	Total
	Butterfly Collection				
		Beautiful Demise	K.D. Harris	$13.99	
		Scarred	K.D. Harris	$13.99	
		Pressure (Coming April 2017)	K.D. Harris	$13.99	
		Dying to Fit In (Coming June 2017)	K.D. Harris	$13.99	
		Legacy (Coming August 2017)	K.D. Harris	$13.99	
		Classy Clique (Coming Sept. 2017)	K.D. Harris	$13.99	
		Caged Secrets (Coming Nov. 2017)	K.D. Harris	$13.99	
		Messy Media (Coming Dec. 2017)	K.D. Harris	$13.99	
	SKP Erotica				
	978-1-944151-04-1	Beyond Measure	K.D. Harris	$15.00	
	978-1-944151-06-5	Beyond Measure II	K.D. Harris	$15.00	
	978-1-944151-62-1	Beyond Measure III (April 2017)	K.D. Harris	$15.00	
	978-1-944151-08-9	The Games We Play	K.D. Harris	$15.00	
	978-1-944151-02-7	For The Love Of It	K.D. Harris	$15.00	
	Eric B Crime Novels				
	978-1-944151-20-1	That Was Dirty	Wasiim	$15.00	
	978-1-944151-22-5	It Gets Dirtier	Wasiim	$15.00	
	978-1-944151-24-9	As Dirty As It Gets	Wasiim	$15.00	
	978-0-9799556-8-6	Money and Murder	Fred Brown	$15.00	
	978-1-944151-35-5	Money and Murder II	Fred Brown	$15.00	
	978-1-944151-39-7	Money and Murder III	Fred Brown	$15.00	
	978-1-944151-49-2	Scandalous Ties	Jermaine "Ski" Buchanan	$15.00	
	978-1-944151-51-5	Scandalous Ties II	Jermaine "Ski" Buchanan	$15.00	
	978-1-944151-52-2	Scandalous Ties III	Jermaine "Ski" Buchanan	$15.00	
	978-1-944151-55-3	Scandalous Ties IV	Jermaine "Ski" Buchanan	$15.00	
	978-0-9799556-2-4	Courts in the Streets	Kevin Bullock	$15.00	
	978-0-9822515-5-3	Courts in the Streets II	Kevin Bullock	$15.00	
	978-1-944151-43-0	Courts in the Streets III	Kevin Bullock	$15.00	
	Total Books Ordered			Quantity	
				Subtotal	

SHIPPING/HANDLING (Via U.S. Priority Mail)		
$7.20 for 1st book, $2.00 for each additional book		
Institutional Check & Money Orders ONLY	Shipping	
(No Personal Checks Accepted)	Total	
Total		$